# The Warrior's Daughter

Blue Moon Book 3

**Alexa Phoenix**

Copyright © 2022 Alexa Phoenix

All rights reserved.

# *Chapter 1*
## Megan's POV

"I can't believe you actually agreed to go, this is amazing." Wes beamed at me; his smile so big it showed his teeth.

"It's not like I'm going because I want to, what else could I say."

Wes rolled his eyes at me.

"Exactly, the Luna personally invited you, how cool is that."

Shaking my head, I give up. I can't win this argument. To Wes going to some pack party is the most exciting thing to ever happen.

There was absolutely no way to convince him otherwise. Shuffling through my wardrobe, trying in vain to find shoes to match the Luna's dress.

"This is useless, I have nothing to match it."

"Oh, hell no, you are not getting out of this. You finally agreed to go."

Wes stood his ground, hand on his hips. Eyebrows raised as he waited for me to argue.

There really is no point.

*Enjoy yourself, we deserve some fun.* My wolf purred.

We have always been so different I sometimes

wonder how we can possibly be one.

It's just a party…

*Well then it should be easy…*

Wes stood up and ran out of the door.

Moments later he rushes back in, bright silver heels in his hand. Raising a brow at him, he just shrugged.

"Stole them from Annie, she won't even notice. Now hurry up and get dressed."

Rolling my eyes, I do as he says. Smirking as I turn to him.

"I forgot to mention, I have a plus one."

His eyes widen, mouth drops open and he growls at me.

"And you waited until now to tell me? Oh, my goddess, I have nothing to wear." raising my eyebrow, my hands fell to my hips as I wait for him to stop freaking out.

"We both know you have something to wear."

He huffs at me.

"Nothing new, I can't go to the Alpha and Luna's engagement party in old clothes." I rolled my eyes again before turning to the mirror applying makeup as he huffs behind me.

"It's a masquerade, no one's going to know it's you."

"I'll know." He grumbled before storming out of

the room.
Ignoring him I turned back to the mirror.
The dress was beautiful, and hugged every curve I had. The baby blue fabric made my caramel skin pop. Even my brown eyes looked brighter.
I silently thanked the Luna for sending it to me. Her note replaying in my head, making me smile.

*Megan,*
*Saw this and thought of you. Please come to this ball, I need back up!*
*Love Andy x*

*Ps: a plus one is totally approved, I'm going to need an army.*

Thirty minutes later and Wes was running back in the room, in a perfectly fitting blur tux. A blue mask covering his face, his short brown hair slicked back.
"Nothing to wear?" I teased as he rolled his eyes at me. Bowing slightly, he reached out an arm to me.
"My lady?"
Giggling I took his hand, and we walked outside. Getting in his truck before driving to the pack house.
They had out done themselves. Lanterns lined the

drive up to the house, all the way to the ballroom. The ballroom was lit with the most beautiful tealights, covering the walls. Everything about it looked right out of a fairy-tale. Eyes landed on me and Wes as we walked in, making me eternally grateful for the mask covering my face.

"I can't believe we're here." Wes whisper yelled in my ear. I couldn't help but smile at my friend, he was so excited.

The Luna and alpha were both on the far side of the room to us, laughing with the beta and his mate.

Andy looked stunning, her purple ballgown flowed around her as she walked, seemingly weightless. Wes clutched my hand, pulling me towards the dance floor.

"What are you doing? You know I can't dance." I whined as he pulls me to him. His arm wrapping around my waist.

He was always a good dancer, me on the other hand was awful. After few minutes of me clumsily tripping over my feet and Wes laughing at me, I finally gave up.

Untangling myself from him, he chuckled again, pulling me closer. I stared at him confused but he just smirked at me before lifting me up and placing me on his feet.

"I'm not five." I whined.

"Maybe, but you dance like a five-year-old."

I stuck my tongue out at him, which only made him laugh harder.

We stayed on the dance floor for what felt like hours before the smell of orange and pine trees brushed over me, making me freeze.

"You, okay?" Wes whispered.

No, please be wrong.

My wolf started howling in my head and I knew exactly what her next words were going to be.

*Mate!* She yipped excitedly.

I felt eyes on my back, as footsteps approached me.

Wes was staring at me, worry covering his features. He pulled me closer to him as the footsteps got closer.

A growl sounded behind me, sending a shiver down my spine. Wes bowed his head, his wolf submitting to him.

The stranger went to grab my hand, Wes reluctantly released me, stepping back. His eyes glued to mine the whole time.

*Sorry.* He whispered through the link.

I gave him a small smile, not trusting my voice, mental or otherwise.

The stranger took my hand, sparks erupted on my

skin as he turned me around.

*Not a stranger, our MATE.* My wolf growled at me.

He is a stranger; do you know his name?

She huffed but stayed silent.

His hand went to my waist as he swayed, holding me against him.

I could feel his eyes burning holes in my skin, but I couldn't bring myself to look at him.

After a few seconds of silence, he reached out, putting his finger under my chin. Lifting my head forcing me to look at him.

My eyes connected with his beautiful grey ones; the rest of the world faded away as we stared at each other.

His face was half covered in a black mask but what I could see was gorgeous. From his black hair slicked back from his face to his strong jawline. He was at least a foot taller than me, in a black tux.

But those eyes...

They're mesmerizing, almost like a thunderstorm. Endlessly powerful, getting lost in them would be way too easy.

His hand goes to his face, and he removes his mask. My breath hitches in my throat as his face comes into full view.

It can't be.

He smiles at me as he reaches out to my face. My

senses come back as his fingers graze my face,
going to take my mask off.
Without thinking I turn and run.
Ignoring my wolfs howls or the growling coming
from behind me.
He can't be my mate.
Grayson O'Connor cannot be my mate.

## *Chapter 2*
Andy's POV

"Are you sure this isn't too much?" Verity asked for the tenth time today. We had decided to go shopping for dresses, my engagement party is on Saturday and it's a formal ball. It's the twenty first century, who has ball's anymore and who has a ballgown just sitting there...

We had gone shopping a couple of times in the past few weeks since Verity joined the pack, every time she would get uncomfortable about us buying her things.

"Verity, just accept the clothes. It truly isn't a bother. It makes Alexi happy to treat his mate."

She sighed before nodding and taking the beautiful green gown to the checkout. Thankfully finding a dress had proved easy, this time. I bought the first one I found; it was exquisite. A light purple that flowed out from my body.

We both headed to a restaurant, starving. Grayson happily carrying the bags as he followed. Ever since I got pregnant, logan's gotten extremely protective. He tried to have a group of warriors following me about, that did not go down well. Eventually I won the argument reminding him I could take all of them. I mean I literally train them. He looked so defeated however that I agreed to Grayson, Alexi or him accompanying me whenever I left the pack grounds.

Today was Grayson's turn. Despite spending the day dress shopping, he hasn't remotely complained. In fact, he's been following us with a smile plastered on his face all day.

Once we were all seated, waiting for our food, curiosity finally got the better of me.

"Why are you so happy, Gray?"

He turned to me, raising an eyebrow, his smile never faltering.

"I guess, it's contagious."

He chuckled when I just raised an eyebrow at him.

"There is just something in the air, you two both have your mates. That just leaves me." He shrugged.

"Are you excited?" Verity asked, her curiosity spiking as well.

His smile grew even more as he thought for a second before answering.

"I can't wait."

They both started discussing Grayson's mate, who she may be, what she might be like. My thoughts however drifted to my mate.

By the time the party came around, my nerves had almost completely dissipated. Aside from a nervous stomach, which I'm putting down to pregnancy. I was actually looking forward to celebrating. I had so much to celebrate, so much to look forward to and be grateful for.

My hand rests on my stomach as I walk towards the ballroom. Popcorn and chocolates filling the air as my mate walks over to join me.

His eyes trailing over my body, darkening as they watch me.

"You look stunning, little one." He said, taking my hand in his.

My cheeks redden and I know I must look like a tomato, but I don't care. In this moment everything is perfect, I have my mate on my arms, a pup in my belly. Everything is amazing.

Tonight, is going to be perfect.

An hour later and the party was in full swing, the dance floor was filled with people dancing and laughing. Logan hadn't left my side all night, his arm remained around my waist, his hand subtly resting on my stomach. Apart from family, no one knew about the pup yet, though an announcement is happening tonight.

"Where's Grayson?" Alexi asked, pulling me from my thoughts.

He was right though; I hadn't seen Grayson all night.

"He wanted to check on the patrols, he should be here any minute." Logan said.

Alexi nodded, pulling Verity to the dance floor as she giggled at him.

"Ready?" Logan whispered.

Nodding I followed him to the stage, my hand resting on my stomach the entire time.

Logan clears his throat, causing the whole room to silence.

"Thank you all for joining us to celebrate." The crowd starts cheering until Logan silences them again.

"We actually have an announcement. We're having a pup!"

The room erupted into chaos, a hundred wolves cheering. Logan pulled me into his side, his face filled with pride as he looked at his pack.

Wolves surrounded us as we left the stage, congratulating us.

The most surprising being the last wolf who came up. A small smile on his face as he nodded his head to us.

"Congratulations Luna." Damon said, not a hint of anger or hate in his eyes.

We hadn't spoken much since the rogue attack, but

I had been curious if our truce was still alive.
Apparently, it is.
A smile lit up my face as I thanked him, he reached out a hand to me, a smirk on his face.
"Care for a dance, Luna?"
I felt Logan tense behind me, I squeezed his hand reassuringly before letting go and letting Damon led me to the dance floor.
His hand landed on my waist as he pulls me closer.
I could practically feel Logan glaring at him.
Damon's eyes shifted behind me before smirking.
"I wouldn't advise annoying him."
His smirk only grew as he looked at me.
"Very true, but it's just so fun."
A growl came from behind us making Damon chuckle.
I turned to leave and go back to my mate, but he spun me back around.
"I apologize Luna, I swear, I meant no offence."
Yeah sure, no offence. Just trying to anger my mate. Why on earth would that be offensive.
"Why are we dancing? Beside angering my mate?"
Damon's eyes softened as he spun me around.
"I wanted to apologize."
My eyes widened as I stared at him, his face showing nothing but raw honesty.
"I shouldn't have blamed you, for what happened

to him." A flicker of pain shot through his eyes before he covered it.

"You're forgiven."

He froze staring down at me, his eyes searching my face, jaw hanging open.

"Just like that? Even after everything?"

"Yes."

"Why?" He whispered.

I looked up at him, our eyes connecting.

"Because I know what it's like, to need someone to blame."

For the longest time he just stared at me, his eyes searching mine before he sighed.

"You truly are a Luna, and entirely too forgiving. But thank you."

"Don't thank me yet, you've missed a lot of training. I expect you there bright and early tomorrow."

He chuckled again and we both started dancing.

"You have my word, Luna."

Growling echoed through the room and we both turned to see Grayson running through the dance floor.

Damon raised an eyebrow at me, I just shrugged, and we both turned and chased after him.

By the time we reached him, he was outside frozen in place, staring at the empty forest in front of him.

Damon was scanning the area around us, searching for the danger. But there was no one else out here. He looked at me confused, his face full of questions.

Shaking my head I walked over to Grayson, placing my hand on his shoulder.

"Gray? What happened? Who were you chasing?"

He turned to face me, his eyes watering as he stared. A gasp involuntarily left my lips, my hand going to my mouth.

I have never seen Grayson look anything other than happy, even when he was in the hospital, but he just looked broken.

"What happened?"

"S-she ran." He stuttered.

"Who? Who ran?"

"My mate."

## *Chapter 3*
Megan's POV


As soon as I pushed through the main doors I paused, unsure of what to do next. There's no way I can outrun him, let alone in these stupid heels. I almost screamed in happiness when Wes's blue truck screeched to a halt in front of me.
Jumping in I yelled at Wes, just as Grayson busted though the doors.
"Drive!"
Wes didn't miss a beat, slamming on the pedal and speeding off leaving Grayson standing at the door. I felt my wolf growl in my head, trying to get me to turn around but I just blocked her out.
"How did you know?" I asked Wes once my breathing had levelled out.
"I saw you, you wanted to run. Thought I'd be the getaway driver." He smiled at me.
"Thank you."
"Always, now why are we running?"
"I met my mate."
The car immediately stopped, the seatbelt almost chocking me from the impact.
"And you ran from him?" He screamed.
When he went to put the truck in reverse I grabbed

his hand, stopping him.

"You know I can't." I pleaded with him.

His eyes softened.

"Not this again Megs, I've told you before it doesn't mean anything. He's your mate."

My head fell in my hands, as the sobs finally started escaping.

"You know it's not that simple. I-I can't so it." I whispered between sobs.

Wes's arms went around me, pulling my head to rest on his shoulder. For the longest time we just sat there in silence, as my tears drenched his shirt. When I finally pulled away, he was staring at me worriedly.

"Are you sure?"

I nodded and he sighed, starting the truck again.

"I want it on record I don't agree with this." I nodded, keeping my eyes out of the window.

"But I'm on your side, Megs. Always." A smile graced my lips, and I was eternally grateful for my best friend. He's always been there, by my side since we were pups.

My eyes fall back to the window, watching the trees pass by as my eyes start to feel heavier.

My eyes opened to sunlight streaming through my window. Stretching, my hand smacks something solid and I hear groaning. Turning I see Wes sprawled out on the bed, his hand cupping his red cheek.

"You hit me?" he whined.

"It was an accident."

He glared at me.

"I carried your ass to bed, and you hit me?"

"You're a werewolf, I'm not that heavy."

"Sure, you're not." He mumbled, getting up.

Did he just call me fat?

Bitch.

Grabbing a pillow I threw it at him, smirking when it hit his head.

"I am not fat."

He looked me dead in the eye and just uh huh me…

Grabbing another pillow, I eyed him. "Take it back."

"Never." He yelled running out the room.

"Coward." I screamed at him.

When I stepped out of bed, realization hit me, I'm in my pajamas. Who the hell undressed me?

"Did you change my clothes?" I yelled at Wes, who was cooking in the kitchen.

"I had to; you would have ruined that dress sleeping in it."

I just stared at him, my mouth hanging open.

"Oh, stop worrying, you're not my type." He was right of course, being that Wes was 100% gay. But

the thought of him changing me felt weird, something felt different somehow.
*Because he's not our mate* my wolf growled at me.
Grayson's face filled my head, how can he be my mate?
"Earth to Megan!" Wes yelled, his hands waving in front of my face.
"Did you say something?" he rolled his eyes at me, plating up some breakfast for us.
"I said, who is he?" he asked as he sat on a stool opposite me.
I took a deep breath before responding. "Grayson O'Connor."
Wes started choking on his food, coughing as he tried to breath.
"G-Grayson... as in gamm-ma Grayson?" he stuttered.
I just nodded.
"Who gives up Grayson freaking O'Connor!" he all but screamed at me.
"That boy is the finest peace of ass in this pack!" a growl involuntarily slipped from my lips causing Wes to raise an eyebrow at me.
Before he could say anything, the kitchen door opened as my father walked in, he smiled at me before rolling his eyes at Wes.
"Don't you have your own house, Weston? Why is

it you are always at mine?"

"Because yours is so much nicer Mr Clarke. Besides, you know you'd miss me."

My father grunted at him as he went to leave, a small smile played at his lips. He had always liked Wes, after Wes's dad first started ignoring him, he had come here. Ever since he's been like family. Wes spends most of his time here, avoiding his parents at all costs, his dad is a dick. Thinks if he ignores it and never lets Wes say the words out loud then he doesn't have a gay son.

"Don't get into trouble you two, oh Megan. Don't forget you agreed to help with the party clean up." And with that he walked out the door to morning training.

"You realize as soon as you walk in that packhouse he's going to smell you?" Wes spoke up.

He was right of course; he would be able to sense the mate bond when I was around.

"I have an idea about that." I whispered.

Wes just stared at me waiting.

"This is such a bad idea." Wes whined for the twentieth time in the last hour. As soon as I told him my plan he started freaking out, I don't blame him. It's a really crappy plan.

"Nothing involving that woman is ever a good

idea." Sighing I fiddled with the necklace I had taken from my father's room.

"How do you even know it works?" he questioned, never taking his eyes off the gem that hung off the chain.

"Because it worked for her, it just didn't do what she wanted."

He glared at me as I clipped the necklace on, the gemstone fell between my chests. A stinging sensation spread across my chest and up my arms.

"Megan?" Wes said, shaking my shoulders.

"Yeah?" he pulled me in for a hug, before pulling away to look at me.

"You zoned out, I don't like this."

"Me either but I need to do it."

He groaned. "Why? If you don't want him, why not just reject him? Why go through all of this?"

Sighing I sat down on the couch, pulling my knees to my chest.

"I just need time; I need to think." I whispered.

He pulled me to his chest, wrapping his arms around me.

"Okay then, but don't forget that thing only works from a distance. If he touches you, he will feel the bond."

"I know, thank you Wes."

He smiled down at me before lifting me onto my

feet.

"Let's get you ready and I'll give you a ride."

I nodded following him upstairs.

This is going to be a long day.

# *Chapter 4*
Grayson's POV

Beep...
Beep...
Groaning I hit my alarm, adding too much force as it shatters into a hundred pieces. Sitting up I lean my back against the headboard. The events of last night replaying in my head.

*I had gotten to the party late. As soon as I entered the ballroom the scent of honey and wildflowers overwhelmed me, almost making my mouth water. My wolf started howling as I searched the room, when my eyes fell on the most beautiful girl I have ever seen, one word echoed through me.*
*Mate!*
*I didn't hesitate, I walked over to her. She kept he back to me as a guy pulled her closer to him.*
*She's ours. My wolf growled.*
*When his hand tightened on her waist a growl slipped from my lips.*
*A sense of satisfaction came over me as he bowed, his wolf submitting easily.*
*Reaching out I grabbed her hand, sparks erupting on my skin from the contact. Swaying around the*

*dance floor, I kept her as close as possible, begging her to look at me, begging to see her face.*

*But her eyes remained trained on the floor. The urge to see her was too much and I reached out lifting her face forcing her to look at me.*

*My eyes connected with her beautiful chocolate brown ones, and everything around us melted away.*

*A white mask covered most of her face, leaving only her eyes and mouth on show. Goddess she's beautiful.*

*I can feel her nervousness so I take my mask off thinking me going first would ease her nerves.*

*I was wrong.*

*As soon as she saw my face her eyes widened, and she froze.*

*As I reached out to grab her mask she turned and runs away. Leaving me standing in the middle of the dance floor.*

*Follow her you idiot" my wolf growls.*

*Not waiting another second, I chase her, trying to get through the thick crowd. Eventually having to growl so the crowd will move. When I reach the door, I see her get into a truck, speeding away. Not even looking back at me.*

*What just happened?*

How did I get here?
Why did she run from us, what if she rejected us?
My wolf howled in my head; he had been quiet since she left.
Groaning, I got out of bed, training started soon, and I'm supposed to be teaching with Andy.

Ignoring the stares of people around me, I sprint to the arena. Having to dodge a few she wolfs on the way, who as they put it 'could help me forget about that bitch.' They backed away once my wolf surfaced, eager to rip them apart for insulting our mate.
Overnight I had become the talk of the pack, everyone seemed to have their own opinion, advice or theory as to what happened. I tried my best to tune them out. However, some people were way to loud about it, the current theory was that she rejected me because of my rank. Because I am not an alpha, nor am I even a beta, I have to admit that one stung.

As soon as I entered the arena it went silent, every wolf turning to look at me. Keeping my eyes trained to the ground I walked towards Andy who was in a heated argument with Damon, her hands on her hips as she glared at him.

"Die hard is not a Christmas movie!" she yelled at him.
Are they really talking about Christmas? It's not even Halloween yet...
Damon rolled his eyes at her.
"Yes, it is, it's set at Christmas. That makes it a Christmas movie."
Andy groaned, throwing her hands in the air.
A triumphant smile covered Damon's face as he watched her give up.
A laugh left my lips as I watched the two. Almost overnight they had gone from enemies to friends. The shift was impressive but not entirely shocking. It's hard not to like Andy.
Andy's head whipped around, turning her glare on me.
As soon as her eyes connected with mine, they softened.
She walked towards me wrapping her arms around me. Her vice like grip not allowing me to pull away. Not that I wanted to, I let myself lean on her, in this moment I needed it. I needed a friend and the time we had spent together recently has mad Andy one of my closest friends. I had been tasked to guard her whilst she was pregnant and it had become my favorite thing, we would go to town and just wonder until we found something to do.

Even though I know Logan forces her to take me along a part of me holds hope that she now chooses to invite me along.

She gave me her biggest smile before pulling me towards Damon. Keeping her arm wrapped around mine as she spoke.

"Take everyone for a run to warm up, five miles should do it."

Damon nodded before leading everyone out of the arena. Once the room was cleared, she turned to me, her smile faltering slightly.

"You doing okay Gray?"

I let out a deep breath, sitting on one of the benches side-lining the field. Andy joined me, sitting sideways, legs crossed facing me.

She watched me patiently, giving me time to consider my answer.

"No." I whispered.

Her hand went to my shoulder, squeezing slightly.

"She ran, she took one look at my face and ran away. Getting in a car with some guy." My voice rose as I spoke, my anger fueling my voice.

"She didn't even look back. And now the entire pack won't shut up, half are throwing themselves at me whilst the other half are laughing. I can't take it. The whole pack knows, everyone I know. My mother! Oh, goddess this is going to kill her, she was so excited to meet my mate. What am I going to tell her?"

When I'd gotten everything out, I turned to Andy. Her eyes were glued to mine as she thought through her answer.

After what felt like an eternity, she stood, wrapping her arms around me before she replied.

"We don't know her reasons Gray before you jump to any conclusions you need to talk to her. As for the pack, ignore them, if anyone so much as looks at you, they'll have me to answer to."

I couldn't help the chuckle that left my lips, causing her to smirk at me before she continued.

"As for your mother, she loves you. She will understand whatever you decide."

Before I could respond the doors swung open as the warriors flooded in.

"Thank you." I whispered, as we headed towards the group of wolves.

Training went by quickly. Andy choosing to go easy on everyone, knowing they were all paying for last night. The whole pack looked rough, from their pale faces to the uncombed hair.

Too much were wine.

Andy looked like Andy, not surprising with the pregnancy.

By the time it was done everyone happily went their separate ways. Thankful to have finished, I on the other hand wasn't looking forward to not having anything to do. I was thankful for the distraction.

I packed up the arena, taking my time. Wanting to stay as busy as possible.

Andy smiled at me as she walked towards the door, waving a goodbye.

When everything was packed away, no more excuses to hide out here left I went back to the packhouse. Ignoring all the stares as I walked towards the packhouse, keeping my eyes fixed on the ground as I walked.

It wasn't until someone screamed that I looked up. Verity was screaming as one of the chandeliers that had been hung from the ceiling for the party started to fall.

Above a girls head...

The girl wasn't moving, her eyes were locked on Verity.

Jumping, my body knocked against the chandelier inches before it touched her.

My body collided with the ground in a thump.

That's definitely going to leave a bruise.

I turned to look at the girl, checking for any signs of injury. As I stepped closer to her, she took a step away. Her eyes wide as she stared at me. Her eyes shifted to the smashed chandelier.

"Thank you." She stuttered, her fingers playing with a gem hanging from her neck.

Verity came rushing over, checking the girl for injury's.

"Megan, I am so sorry. I pulled the wrong string."

The girl, Megan. Just smiled at her.

"It's okay, I'm fine."

Verity instantly calmed, but her eyes shifted to the pile of rubble that was the chandelier and she looked uneasy.

After a moment of awkward silence, Megan pulled Verity towards the mess.

"Come on, let's get it cleaned up."

Verity nodded and they walked off. Megan keeping her eyes trained on the floor the entire time.

Why did that frustrate me so much?

I don't even know this girl.

I paused, watching them. Unsure of what to do next. Deciding to ignore the strange feeling, I turned and headed to my room.

## *Chapter 5*
### Megan's POV

I watched Grayson leave, ignoring the ache in my chest to follow him.
How did I end up here?
Everything is so screwed up.
The gem around my neck heated up as Grayson came in, now the stone was finally cooling down. Leaving a small red mark on my chest.
Verity pulled my attention as she struggled to lift the broken light, grunting with the effort.
Smiling I reached out, grabbing the other side and helped her lift it.
Once all the wood and glass had been cleared, verity went back to work on the rest of the decorations.
I watched her for a second before turning to leave.
Five minutes.
I just need five minutes to breath and clear my head. After a few moments I finally made it outside, fresh air filling my lungs.
I felt myself start to calm as I lent on the cold brick building.
I don't know how long I stood there, eyes closed, taking slow cold breaths.

The Warrior's Daughter

Jumping at Andy's voice, the sound so close it caused me to yelp.
"Are you okay?"
After a pause of silence, me gasping, trying to calm my racing heart. Andy just leaned on the building beside me, patiently waiting.
"I'm fine, just needed some air."
Andy raised an eyebrow at me, waiting for me to continue but I couldn't. She wouldn't understand, none of them would. They hadn't lived through it like I had. They couldn't understand it.
When I remained silent Andy sighed, walking towards the door. Looking over her shoulder she said.
"Come with me."
Bowing my head I followed her inside, expecting her to head into the ballroom. But she didn't, instead she turned and started walking upstairs. Silently motioning me to follow her.
We walked to the third floor and sown the long hallway before reaching the alpha's suite.
"I thought you'd prefer to speak in private, besides Logan's been frustratingly protective lately and I told him I was going to rest for a while. I dread to think of the fuss that man would make if he came here, and I was elsewhere "she said chuckling slightly at the thought.

She settled on the bed, tapping the empty spot beside her. After hesitating for a moment, I say down, she's the Luna and she's Andy, there's really no point in arguing.

"I really am fine Lu..." she glared at me. "I mean Andy, I promise. I just needed some air; besides, I am supposed to be cleaning up the ballroom."

"That dress I bought; it suited you perfectly last night. You looked stunning."

I smiled, thanking her.

My face paled as realization dawned on me, she had seen my dress. She had bought it, even with the mask on she would have known it was me.

I turned to look at her, she was smirking at me.

"You know, don't you?"

"I saw you dancing with a man, when Grayson ran, I didn't see who he was chasing. But he described his mate, and when we went back inside you were nowhere to be found. It wasn't hard to piece it together."

She knew, the whole time.

"You haven't told him." I didn't phrase it as a question, but she shook her head anyway.

"Why?" I whispered.

"I have some understanding of rejection." She smiled; her eyes sad as she continued.

"It is not my place to force you into anything,

besides, I do not believe you would run without a reason to do so."

Keeping my eyes fixated on my hands, avoiding her gaze as it burned a hole in the side of my head.

"I, I can't do it."

Andy was quiet for a moment before she spoke.

"Now, or forever?"

Burying my head in my hands, I began to sob.

"I-I'm not sure." I stuttered between sobs.

Her arms wrapped around me, bringing my face to her shoulder. We both stayed like that for what felt like hours, me crying on her shoulder and her chin resting on my head. Until my tears dry up and I pulled away wiping my eyes.

"I do not enjoy lying to my friend." She whispered.

When I went to apologize, she shook her head. Silencing me.

"However, I will not expose you."

Shocked, my eyes found hers.

She wouldn't tell him.

Why?

"I won't tell him, however if he asks me directly, I won't lie to him."

Nodding, I smiled at her. Thankfully, she was being so kind to me.

"He's a good guy, you know?" She finally whispered.

A knock on the door pulled our attention.

"Come in." Andy yelled.

After a second, the door opened, and Verity walked in.

"Logan said you'd be up here. Oh, hi Megan, are you okay?"

"She's fine, just needed to talk. Is everything okay?"

She nodded. "Yeah, the boys were just being annoying. I needed somewhere to hide."

Andy chuckled, moving over slightly. Making room for Verity on the bed.

Verity sprawled out on the foot of the bed, groaning when someone knocked on the door.

Verity shuffled, crawling off the bed and hiding behind it.

"Come in." Andy yells, chuckling at Verity's glare towards the door.

A second later Grayson opened the door. His eyes falling on us, a confused look on his face.

Andy's gaze shifted between us; her eyes filled with questions.

"Have you seen Verity?"

"Nope, is something wrong?"

Grayson shuffled on his feet, his hand running through his hair.

"What did you do?" Andy groaned.

His cheeks tinted red as he avoided her gaze.
"Alexi thought she might be able to help, I think I may have phrased it badly though."
"Phrased what?" Andy persisted.
"If she knew my mate because well, she..."
"Please tell me you didn't ask her because she ran too."
Grayson groaned, still avoiding eye contact.
"I'll talk to her." Andy said, shooing him away.
As soon as the door closed Verity jumped up, back on the bed.
"So, he asked you about running, and your response was to run?" Andy asked, keeping her face calm. She was struggling to keep a straight face when Verity shrugged. She broke and burst out laughing.
"I never said it was a smart plan." Verity groaned, making Andy laugh even more.
My restraint broke and I started laughing as Andy struggled to speak between laughing fits.
"His face, he looked terrified."
"You should've seen him when I ran, his mouth dropped open."
The door swung open, and Alexi walked in, staring at all of us.
"You could knock." Andy groaned.
"I could... have you seen Grayson? I think he's

avoiding me."

"Why would you think that?" Verity asked.

"I yelled to him, but he just paled and ran in the other direction."

Andy, Verity and me all locked eyes and burst into a hysterical laughing fit.

"Have I missed something? Again?" Alexi whined, sounding more like a toddler than a beta.

Our laughter only got louder as he glared at us, mumbling a whatever as he left the room.

## *Chapter 6*
Andy's POV

Once Megan and Verity left, I collapsed on the bed exhausted.
This was all a lot easier before I was pregnant.
Falling asleep before my head even reached the pillow.

The next afternoon, once training was finished, I curled up on my bed, a book in my hands. I made it through two pages before my mother mind-linked me, interrupting my me time.
*Andrea, we need you downstairs.*
A nap.
All I wanted was a nap.
I'm growing a person here.
Groaning I pulled myself out of bed, walking downstairs. The sound of my mother's voice filled my ears before I even reached the bottom step.
"We need at least fifty of these to start."
As I turned the corner, I held back a laugh as I watched my mother order around an Omega, who was struggling with a pile of boxes as he followed her.
"Mother, stop over working the poor boy."

My mother dismissed him, and walked towards me. The omega mouthed a thank you before running in the other direction.
"What are you doing mother?"
"We have a baby shower to plan."
My stomach dropped as she smirked at me.
"Let's get started, first we need a theme, then we have to decide on the gender reveal, and food, guests, dates."
Goddess saves me.
My wolf whined as we followed our mother, listening to all her plans.

Three hours later I finally escaped party planning. Finally escaped my mother.
Goddess I'm starving, keeping out of sight, I made my way to the kitchen. Desperate for something edible.
Megan stood at the sink, her focus on the stack of dishes beside her.
"Hey Megan." I said, veering to the fridge.
Sighing with relief as I spotted the container of leftover pasta.
"Good afternoon, I can make you something fresh if you like?" she asked, glaring at the tub of cold pasta.
Ignoring her, I started eating. Savoring every bite.

"I'm good, do you want a hand?"

Megan looked at me shocked, quickly shaking her head.

"No, goddess no. It's my job. You're the Luna, you shouldn't be doing dishes."

Rolling my eyes I grabbed a towel, drying as Megan washed. For a while we stayed like that, until Megan grabbed a pile of clean dishes carrying them towards the dining room.

It wasn't until I heard growling that I chased after her.

Megan was standing in the entrance of the door, her hands fisted as she glared out the window.

Following her gaze, I saw Grayson talking to a she wolfs. She was laughing as her hand rested on his arm.

She's flirting with him.

Another growl slipped from Megan as she watched them, her eyes shifting to black.

Not Megan.

Her wolf is in control.

She inched closer to the window, bracing herself as she glared.

Before she could lunge out of the window to attack the unsuspecting girl. I grabbed her shoulders, hiding her back.

She struggled against me, growling as my grip got

tighter.

Using my Alpha tone, I said. "Stop, control your wolf." Trying my best to keep my voice calm. Not an easy feat, considering she was kicking out at me. My words calmed her though, she relaxed in my arms. Her eyes going back to their natural colour as she glared at the woman.

"I... I'm sorry Luna."

I released her, stepping between her and the window. Blocking her view.

"Come on, let's go upstairs." I whispered, grabbing her hand and leading her to my room.

Before we even made it to the stairs a brown-haired man ran up to us. He took one look at Megan and wrapped his arms around her.

"What happened Meg?"

Megan gave a humorless laugh before whispering. "Some she wolfs had her hands all over him and I reacted."

The guy growled before shifting his eyes to me. He bowed his head.

"I'm sorry Luna."

"Andy, call me Andy."

Megan looked between us smiling at her red-faced friend.

"Andy, this is Wes."

Wes smiled at me; his eyes shifted between the

two of us.
"Stop worrying, she knows about Grayson."
He sighed, his whole body relaxing.
"Thank goddess, I'm a terrible liar."
Chuckling we carried on upstairs, Wes following behind us.

Once we had all settled in my room, me and Megan sitting on the bed, Wes on the couch opposite us. A few moments of silence passed before Wes jumped up his hands clapping together before he exclaimed.
"We are not going to sit around on our butt's feeling sorry for ourselves over some guy! No matter how fine a man he is."
Megan giggles as Wes jumps on the bed beside us.
"What exactly do you suggest?" Megan challenged.
A ruefully smile covered his face as he stared at the two of us.
"Drinking, dancing. You know, what normal teenagers do!"
"Are you forgetting she's pregnant?"
He shook his head, rolling his eyes at Megan.
"You don't need alcohol to have fun. It just helps."
I couldn't help but smile as I watched the two of them, Megan groaning dramatically as Wes laughed. They reminded me so much of Alexi and

me.

A knock sounded at the door, we all turned to watch Verity walk in. Her face embarrassed as she took in Megan and Wes.

"I... I'm sorry. I didn't realize you had company."

"It's fine Verity, are you okay?"

She sighed, sitting on the bed beside me.

"I love him, I do but I need to escape this packhouse." Megan gasped, watching us.

"No, no. Not like escape, escape."

We all relaxed, as she spoke.

"Just for a breath. I've barely done anything, barely seen anything."

"Well, looks like you're coming with us."

I said, she turned to me. Eyebrow raised in a question.

"Where are we going?"

"Prison break." I replied.

She looked confused, but her eyes lit up with excitement.

"There's only one problem." They all turned to me, patiently.

"I don't have any idea what to wear dancing."

"I can fix that." Wes cheered, his eyes beaming.

## *Chapter 7*
Megan's POV

To say Wes was excited by the idea of dressing the Luna would be the world's biggest understatement. The second we all agreed to his night out he ran out the door, only to return half an hour later with a pile of bags that could rival Everest.

"What exactly did you bring Wes?" I whined as he handed me a worryingly light bag.

He smiled, moved and handed one to Verity before turning to Andy, grabbing a box smiling.

"There is one thing have wanted to do since you became our Luna."

Andy shifted slightly, eyeing him up. Unsure of his intentions.

She groaned as he took out a pair of shiny pink hair straighteners.

"Let's tame those gorgeous locks of yours."

A giggle slipped through my lips as I watched Andy, our powerful Alpha-Luna whine like a pup as Wes brushed her hair.

Before long Verity had slipped into a beautiful green knew length dress. Unfortunately, Wes hadn't been so kind to me, he had chosen a skin-

tight red lace, strapless dress, that barely reached my thighs along with a matching pair of stilettos. Goddess, I'm going to trip and break my neck.
Andy's hair make over was finally finished, her golden hair fell straight cascading over her shoulders and down her back.
"This is your dress." Wes said, handing over the last bag.
Andy smiled gratefully, removing her shirt to slip on the dress. Wes went to help her with the zip as the door opened, a growl echoing through the room.
Logan stood in the doorway, his black eyes glaring at Wes.
Wes's face paled as he took a step away from Andy.
"What the hell is going on?" Logan growled, moving towards a very frightened Wes.
Andy shifted between the two of them she placed her hand on Logans chest, stopping him.
"It's okay handsome."
"Okay! He had his hands on you." He roared.
I took a step back, noticing Verity and Wes doing the same. Andy however just laughed at her mate.
"I do believe you're more his type than me."
Logans eyes flew to her before shifting to Wes. Understanding filled his eyes as they softened. A

small red tinge covering his cheeks as he pulled his mate into his arms.

Logan instant calmed, an adoring smile covering his face as he looked at Andy.

How I envy them, they are perfect for each other, it's obvious from the way they look at each other. Eventually I had to look away, watching them only made my heart ache.

"Where exactly are you, all going?" Logan asked.

Reluctantly I turned my eyes back to them, Logan's eyes trailed Andy. The dress Wes had chosen for her was stunning. The hem just reached the bottom of her thighs as it flowed out. The low v in the front reached the bottom of her ribs, leaving very little to the imagination.

The dark black material made her pale skin glow as she moved. Wes had truly out done himself.

"Dancing." Andy smirked.

Logans hand went to her waist as he leaned towards her.

"Then let's go."

Andy laughed, smacking his arm.

"Girls only handsome."

When Wes whined, Andy corrected herself.

"And Wes."

A massive cheesy grin covered his face as he rushed into the bathroom to get dressed. Logan growled, his eyes darkening as he looked over Andy again.

"Please." He begged.

My hands covered my mouth, trying desperately not to laugh at the whining alpha.

"Nope." Andy replied, popping the P.

Another groan before Logan submitted, kissing her on the cheek before turning to leave. A blush covered Andy's face as she watched him exit. Realizing he must have linked his response I couldn't hold back my laughter anymore.

I think he broke her.

Andy looked almost nervous. I've never seen her like that before. I've never seen her speechless.

"Ready?" Wes asked, emerging from the bathroom. Dressed in grey skinny jeans, with a button up black shirt. I glared at his completely covered form.

So not fair.

We all nodded, following him out of the room.

Well, this should be interesting.

Andy had gotten a warrior to drive us to the club, saying it would be easier. But I knew better, she just wanted to make Logan feel more comfortable. Having a warrior escorting us word definitely do that.

As soon as we had arrived at the club, Wes had headed straight for the bar. Leaving us girls to find a table. Andy ushered us towards the VIP section as one of the bouncers smiled at her.
"Luna." He bowed.
Andy smiled.
"Justin, I didn't know you worked here."
He smiled proudly. "A few of us own the club."
"Follow me, we have a table free in the back."
We all followed him to a secluded booth at the back of the room. Andy smiled, thanking him as we took our seats.
As soon as we were settled Wes came running over, a tray of drinks in his hands.
He placed them in front of us, handing a tall glass to Andy.
"Coke." Wes confirmed as she eyed it. A grateful smile covered her lips as she took a sip. The rest of the tray was filled with shot glasses, all overflowing.
"These are for us, they were friendly." He winked at me as I groaned.
"Time to drink." He cheered, putting two shots in front of me and Verity before grabbing two for himself.
Groaning, I down the drinks. Wincing as my throat burned. There's no point fighting with Wes, I've

known him long enough to know it would be pointless.

"And now, we dance." Wes held out his hands, one to Verity and one to me. I shook my head; Wes rolled his eyes but didn't protest as he led Verity to the dance floor.

"I think those two are cute together." Andy said as we watched them dance. Calling it dancing would be polite. Verity was ungracefully swaying, whilst Wes made a fool of himself. Spinning and twirling, causing Verity to giggle uncontrollably.

That's what I love about my best friend, he would never think twice about embarrassing himself to make you feel more comfortable.

After a comfortable silence, Andy spoke.

"How are you doing?"

"Honestly, I have no idea. My wolf will barely talk to me, Wes is watching me like I'm going to break. I always knew it would be hard, but this is impossible." I turned to face her, tears falling from my eyes as I spoke.

"I miss him, how is that even possible? I barely know him. How can I possibly miss him?"

Andy's eyes softened as she listened, when I finished, she sighed.

"The mate bond is a lot stronger than you expect it

to be, sometimes it can feel like a curse."
Shocked I stared at her. They were so perfect for each other, why would she feel like that.
Andy's eyes widened; she shook her head as she rushed to say.
"Not Logan. Connor, with Connor, I hated it. I hated him, but the bond kept making me want to be around him."
I nodded, feeling stupid for even considering the idea that she had meant Logan.
"You're right sometimes it really feels like a curse."
You have no idea how much.
"He's not a bad guy you know. He'd never hurt you or do anything you didn't want. If that's what you're worried about."
Sighing, I just nodded. Not trusting my voice, I wish that was the problem. I would do anything to be given a choice. But the choice was made for me, a long time ago.
Wes interrupted my thoughts as he placed another tray of shots in front of me.
"Drink, and then we dance." I glared at him, but he just ignored me. Motioning to all three of us.
"We all need to have fun. I swear it's like you forgot you're all eighteen."
Andy giggled, shaking her head.
"I think you may be right, I guess we all skipped the

teenager faze."

Wes nodded his agreement, reaching out a hand for Andy. She smiled, grabbing his hand whilst I grabbed the other.

The four of us walked to the dance floor, Verity leading the way. By the time we reached the crowded platform, the shots had started to take effect.

I felt all the, but up tension slowly leaves my body as I moved to the beat of song after song. Only stopping when Wes brought more shots.

Wes was right, we all needed a night of acting our age.

No mates, no responsibilities, just us.

Verity moaning had us all stopping and turning to her, she was standing on the edge of the dance floor, her eyes wide as she gawked at the front of the club.

Following her eye line, I spotted three familiar faces as they entered the club. All of them dressed in tight fitting jeans and Button up shirts clinging to their firm muscles.

The crowd gave them a wide birth, all the females swooning.

I barely heard Andy mutter.

"Bad alpha." Under her breath.

My eyes were fixed on him.

Grayson walked behind Logan; his eyes trained on the floor. Never once looking up at the crowd around them.

His lips were set in a firm line, his hands fisted at his sides. It took all the self-control I have not to comfort him. It was obvious he didn't want to be here, well obvious to me anyway. No one else seemed to notice.

My wolf whined, she wanted to go to him too.

My heart raced as his head shot up, his eyes searching the club.

Did he hear her?

Crap.

So many emotions passed over his face, I struggled to identify them. Shock, hope, fear, sadness.

Eventually he hung his head, his eyes dulling as he reached us.

Andy's eyes shifted towards me, filled with so many questions.

I could see the struggle in her eyes, she wanted to comfort her friend too. She's our Luna, she's struggling against her instinct for me. I hate that I've put her in this position.

Why couldn't I just be like everybody else.

Why did I have to be like this?

I never chose this!

My anger started to build as I watched my mate in

pain.

Useless, I am useless. All I can bring him is pain.

I felt Wes tense beside me, his arm going around my waist, pulling me towards him.

"Careful Megs, your wolf is showing." He whispered in my ear, the smell of alcohol surrounding me as he spoke.

A growl slipped through Grayson's lips before he straightened himself, shaking his head slightly. His eyes filled with confusion as he stared at me.

*He wants to kill Wes, but he has no idea why.* Andy's voice filled my head.

I vaguely hear Andy and Logan talking, my focus completely on Grayson as his eyes travelled over me. Darkening as he stares.

A giggle leaves Andy's lips, pulling me from my haze, raising an eyebrow at her she just giggles again.

*He's so confused, he can't take his eyes off of you.* Again, she giggles.

*He has a confused boner.* By the time she had finished, she was in hysterics.

All of us watching her as she clutched her chest struggling to breathe.

Grayson growled at her, rolling his eyes before walking over and rubbing his hand through her hair.

Ruining Wes's hard work and making it frizz. Andy whined as she tried to tame her hair.

"So uncalled for." She whined.

He huffed at her as he turned to walk towards the bar.

## Chapter 8
### Grayson's POV

I barely slept last night; every time I closed my eyes my mates eyes filled my vision. The shock, fear and anger in them as she turned and ran.
Everything is so screwed up, I spent last night avoiding my mother. She would ask so many questions, I'm not ready to answer.
I was thankful when Andy led training this morning, allowing me to train with the pack, enjoying the release of all my built-up anger.
By the time training was finished I has already decided to stay behind. Hiding out in the arena, rather than face the pack.

I managed to avoid them until I was almost at the packhouse. One of the she-wolves cornering me, purring as she spoke.
"I've been looking for you, Grayson."
I suppressed the urge to growl as she placed her hand on my arm.
"I thought I could help take your mind off of your mate."
The thought of her touching me made me want to vomit.

A growl distracted me, stopping me from pushing her away.

Who was that?

My wolf whined as he tried to come to the surface, wanting to follow the sound.

Could that have been her?

Our mate?

My eyes refocused as the girl in front of me grabbed my hand, trying to pull me with her.

My wolf growled, causing her to shrink back.

"Leave."

A pout formed on her lips.

"But I..."

"I said leave." I growled; my wolf satisfied as she ran off.

I allowed my wolf cool and felt my heart ache when he couldn't find her. Maybe I'm going crazy.

After my wolf gave me control back, I went upstairs, eager to avoid social interaction for another evening.

A few hours later my door flung open as Logan barged in.

"What are you doing here?"

Logan growled, ignoring me as he went into my closet. Throwing clothes at me as he said.

"Get dressed."

When I didn't move, he growled again.

"We are going out. You're not going to find her lying on your arse."

Growling I stood, grabbing the clothes as I went into the bathroom.

The last thing I need is to go out, why does everyone keep trying to force me into things.

*Because they care?* My wolf growled.

Ignoring him I changed into the jeans and shirt Logan had chosen.

*He is right, you know?*

How?

*We will never find her, hiding up here.*

Sighing I submitted, I couldn't argue with that. They were right.

By the time I made it out of the bathroom Alexi had joined Logan.

"Where exactly are we going?"

Logan smirked.

"Girls night."

Me and Alexi both stared at him before Alexi chuckled.

"I take it you didn't get invited?"

Growling Logan started heading downstairs, both of us following him.

"I'm the alpha, I don't need an invitation."

Alexi laughed again.

"I'm so telling Andy you said that."
Logan visibly paled.
"Don't you dare."

One look at the girls and it was obvious we were definitely not invited.
Verity was shocked, Andy annoyed and the other girl, Megan seemed uncomfortable having us here. For the second time today, I heard growling. My heartbeat picked up and we searched the club but nothing.
She wasn't here.
She was still lost to me. It wasn't until I saw that wolf pull Megan towards him, his mouth going to her ear that I was pulled out of my haze.
My wolf growled at him, urging me to attack.
*Are you okay Gray?* Andy linked me.
*I'm not sure, my wolf is acting strange against him, and I don't know why.*
My eyes shifted to Megan, taking her in.
The red dress hugged her skin, clinging to her curves. I felt my body react to her, wanting her.
*Now he wants Megan! What the hell is wrong with me?* I linked Andy who took one look at me, shifting in my now too tight jeans and burst out laughing.
Damn traitor.

Growling at my so-called best friend I messed up her hair before heading to the bar.
Goddess, I need a drink.

## Chapter 9
Grayson's POV

The guys paired off with their mates, pulling them to the dance floor. Megan leaving them, sitting at a table overlooking the dance floor.
Two shots of whiskey down I took the third as I walked towards the table. Megan stiffened as I sat down, her eyes widening as she watched me.
My wolf still felt on edge, trying to get to the surface.
"Not much of a dancer?"
Megan's eyes shot to me, shifting to black before returning to their natural colour.
A few minutes of silence pass as she plays with the hem of her dress, she speaks.
"Not really, are you?"
"Nah, not really. At least not like that."
Motioning to the drunken mass of people on the dance floor.
A giggle slipped from her lips as Alexi lifted a squealing Verity, twirling her across the dance floor.
Megan watched the pair intently, a sad expression on her face.
"Are you okay?"

Before she could respond Wes placed a tray of drinks in front of us. Dropping in the seat beside Megan, Wes draped an arm over her shoulder.
My hands gripped the table so hard they paled as I stared at them. My wolf was still on edge, stupid animal.
She isn't ours; we have a mate.
The sooner he accepts that the better.
*I will accept nothing.*
Why?
*He's not allowed to touch her!*
If you have a valid reason to be acting like a feral dog, maybe I'll let it go.
Growling, he put up his wall. Blocking me out. Stubborn wolf.
"I need some air."
Turning I watched as Megan stood and headed for the exit.
My feet began to move before I could comprehend what was happening. I was outside, staring at a sobbing Megan.
I watched as she looked up at the sky, tears rolling down her face as she yelled into the air.
"Why are you doing this to me?"
Hesitantly I took a step towards her. Tensing she spun around, her eyes going wide as they landed on me.

"What are you doing here?"
Stopping, I stared at her. Realizing I had no good reason for following her.
"I, um. You were upset."
Her face softened slightly as she stepped towards me.
"I'm fine, I just needed a moment. We best get back."
Her eyes stayed on the ground as she tried to walk past me, holding her arms against her chest.
"I'm sure they'll be fine for a few minutes."
Stopping she turned to me, her eyes searching mine.
With a sigh she walked towards one of the benches.
Her eyes avoiding me as she sat down.
"What happened? Maybe I can help."
She fidgeted with her hands, not answering me.
"You never know, saying it could make it better."
"Not everything."
For a while we just sat there, staring into space. The low hum of the music filling the air.
Wes came running out, his eyes searching the decking. When they landed on Megan, he rushed over to her.
Wrapping his arms around her, as she rested her head on his chest for support.

My hands curled into fists as I watched them, unable to stop myself.

Wes's eyes shot to my hands before rising to meet my eyes.

Mouthing a quick thank you, he ushered Megan back inside. Leaving me sitting alone.

## Chapter 10
Megan's POV

Standing in the middle of a field I waited for something. No idea what I was waiting for. Looking around, stepping toward the trees, I saw something glowing in the dense forest. It was a flicker of something yellowish, almost gold even. Craning to get a better look, but after blinking to clear my eyes a bit, I realized that the glow was no longer there. In its place was a Grayson, dressed in a white shirt and jeans, pristine and fitting tightly over his muscled frame.

His face was dark, hidden in the shadows still, but somehow, I knew it was him.

Slowly I began to move towards him as soon as I was within a few feet of him, he began to move towards me.

His arms embracing me and sending sparks throughout my entire body.

His hands slowly ran over me, tracing my shape as he moved from my breasts down to my hips. His movements were so gentle, despite his size and the width of his hands.

The silk from his shirt rubbing against my skin

under his touch, he moved further down still and squeezed at my ass.

Moving up again he picked me up and brought my face towards his, bringing my lips to his. At first, he was gentle.

As I let out a soft moan, he became more insistent, driving his mouth harder onto mine, reaching down to my breasts and running a thumb over the thin silk covering my erect nipples.

I could feel a firmness pressed against me as he lowered me to the ground.

His hand moved up a few inches from my breasts and grabbed at the neckline of the dress. In one smooth movement he pulled, and the dress clean off as if it was made of tissue.

His hand trailed down my skin until he reached my core.

Ever so slowly his hand moved further, only allowing the very tips of his fingers to enter me, while he looked into my eyes.

His fingers quickened, my body tensing as I was about to...

I jerked awake, my cheeks burning as I realized what just happened.

It was a dream.

It was all a dream.

By the time I reached the packhouse the next day, both Alexi and Logan were leant against the kitchen counter, holding their heads in their hands as they moaned.
Andy chuckled at the pair as she shuffled around the kitchen, grabbing supplies from the fridge and placing them on the counter.
"I told you the 4$^{th}$ round of shots was too many."
Again, the boys moaned, Alexi sticking his tongue out at his sister.
"Where is Verity?"
Alexi turned to Andy, glaring.
"I tried to wake her, she threw a pillow at my head and told me to shut up."
Andy laughed again, shaking her head.
"I'm not surprised, she drank almost as much as you. Has anyone heard from Grayson? I never saw him leave."
Logan nodded, groaning at the pain the movement caused him.
"He left early; I don't think he was up to partying after what happened with his mate."
Alexi sighed.
"I'm not surprised, rejection sucks."
"He hasn't been rejected, at least not yet."
Andy watched the pair argue, her expression thoughtful.

"We don't know what will happen, it is not our place to judge."
Alexi nodded his agreement, but Logan looked unsure.
"She ran away with another guy, pretty clear answer I think."
When Andy glared at him, he continued.
"I'm just saying, he could do better than someone who doesn't even have the decency to reject him. Instead, she leaves him wondering and in pain, when he should be accepting it and moving on."
Andy's eyes went wide as they shot to me.
"Good morning, Megan, I didn't hear you come in."
Both the boys looked towards me, nodding their heads in greeting before resting them on the table again.
"Sorry, I should have knocked or something."
Andy smiled, her eyes softening.
"You're welcome anytime, there's no need to knock."
Her eyes met mine, and I could see the unspoken words in them.
'This is your house too now.'
Trying my best to ignore the melancholy feeling overcoming me, I walked towards her. Staring at the counter covered in ingredients before turning to her.

"What are you making? Perhaps I can help."
"A hangover cure my mother taught me. Its smoothie, we just have to blend all of this together."
Nodding I grabbed a hand full of oranges, peeling and cutting them as Andy grated ginger.
After a few minutes, the smoothies were made, Alexi, me and Logan, all drinking them up. Each of us eager to diminish the pain.
Triumphant Andy started to clean the kitchen, her work as our nurse complete.
"Perhaps you should take one up to Verity, it might help her feel better."
Nodding Alexi picked up a glass, carrying it upstairs towards his mate.
Sitting at the counter, I watched the two mates. Envious of what they had. Andy swayed around the room, Logan watching intently, a smile on his face. They are both so happy, it's painful to watch, knowing I'll never have what they share.
That I could never have that.
"I need to go into town this afternoon, I was thinking you could join me. I doubt Verity is going to be up for baby shopping and I could use the help."
Andy asked, her eyes fixed on me.
"Yeah, sure. I have a few jobs to do, but I should be

able to get through them quickly."
Smiling, Andy went back to cleaning.
"Don't forget you need a guard."
Turning to Logan Andy smirked.
"Well, why don't you join us then handsome."
Logan stood up, pulling her to him. He kissed her, whispering. "I think I'll take you up on that. 1oclock sound, okay?"
"Perfect"
With one last kiss, Logan went to work. Leaving the two of us alone.
Saying a quick goodbye to Andy, I went to work.

By 1oclock, the packhouse was clean and my list completed. I joined Andy as she leant on the front of the packhouse, waiting for Logan.
The smell of orange and pine filled my nose, making me tense. Andy's eyes flew to me, a question forming on her lips. She stopped, her eyes finding something behind me.
"Grayson, what are you doing here?"
"Logan got stuck at work, he asked me to escort you."
Andy's eyebrows furrowed, her gaze shifting to me. With a sad expression, she mouthed a quick sorry. Not wanting to ruin my new friends day, I straightened. Taking a breath to steady myself

before, grabbing her hand and pulling her to the car.

"We best get going then, we've got a busy day ahead."

Squeezing me hand, Andy followed me, smiling. Grayson following a few steps behind.

By the third baby store, my wolf was becoming extremely hard to control. she wanted out, she wanted to close the last few steps between us and Grayson.

Fisting my hands, I let my claws dig into my palm. Trying to keep them from the prying eyes of the humans around us.

"Are you okay?" Grayson whispered, making me jump out of my skin. Spinning, I realized he had walked straight up to me, without me even noticing. No doubt my wolfs doing, distract me so he gets close enough to 'accidentally' touch me and my secret would be out.

Taking a step back, I let my eyes connect with his. His eyes widened and I knew my eyes were dark, my wolf showing.

"I'm fine, my wolf is just acting up."

His eyes shifted to my hands; I knew what he was looking at. A warm line had been travelling across my palm, I had squeezed so tight I broke the skin.

He could smell the blood.

"Perhaps, you should shift. We can drive out of town, somewhere secluded."

"No." I almost yelled, his eyebrows furrowing at my response.

Without thinking I say the first thing that comes to mind.

"She wants her mate."

A sadness fills his eyes as he watches me.

"And that's a problem because?"

"She can't have him, he rejected us." I blurt. My hand rushing to my mouth.

His eyes darken, a growl slipping through his lips.

"I'm sorry." He whispers, his hand reaching out to wipe the tear from my cheek. Flinching, I suppressed a whine at the pained expression on his face.

As he opened his mouth to speak, Andy came over to us. Her eyes shifting between us, questioningly.

"I was thinking, we could grab food. The baby's craving pizza."

Nodding, Grayson turned, leading us towards the closest Italian restaurant.

*Our mate rejected us.* My wolf growled as we sat at an empty seat in the restaurant.

It just slipped out.

"I need to pee, again. Be back in a sec." Andy said

as she rushed to the bathroom.
Leaving me and Grayson alone.
"I'm sorry about before, it wasn't any of my business."
"it's fine really."
Grayson looked unconvinced as he leant over the table, closer to me.
"I should have realized, after last night. I could see it."
"See what?"
His eyes locked on mine, filling with so much emotion I had to look away.
"The pain in your eyes, it's the same in mine I'd imagine. As if a piece of you is missing."
My wolf whined, wanting so much to comfort her mate. It took the last remaining piece of my self-restraint not to wrap my arms around him. To tell him I'm sorry for running, that I accept him. That he's mine.
Instead, I bring my eyes up to meet his, taking a breath to keep my voice steady before I whisper.
"Maybe it's for the best, maybe we don't always deserve a happy ending."

## *Chapter 11*
Megan's POV

Eventually, we all made our way back to the pack house. A car filled with half a baby store, meaning the three of us only just fit in the car.
"Thank you both, I can't believe we managed to get everything in one day." Andy said as we walked inside, Grayson carrying a pile of boxes on one hand, me carrying bags of baby clothes.
"It was no problem, really." I assured her as we piled everything into the nursery.
"Why don't you guys go to the tv room, ill order food as a thank you."
Nodding we leave her to order food, heading downstairs.
As we sat down on the couches Grayson spoke up, his voice serious.
"You're wrong, you know?"
Confused I just stared at him, waiting for him to explain.
"About deserving a happy ending, because you do."
My heart swelled as he spoke, wishing so much I could believe him.

"Sometimes things don't always work like that, sometimes we don't get a say in the matter. Someone else chooses for us."

His eyes were thoughtful as he considered my words.

"Whoever he is, he's an idiot for rejecting you. You deserve better."

Blinking away the tears threatening to fall I looked away from him. Holding myself back from screaming at the universe for doing this to me, to him. he deserved so much more than this, he deserved to move on and be happy. But I'm too weak to even give him that.

"No, I don't, but you do." I whispered as Andy joined us.

Sitting beside me, her eyes found mine. Concern covering her face as she caught sight of the unshed tears. Giving her a small reassuring smile, I turned my attention back to Grayson.

His gaze was unfocused as he ran through his thoughts, a sad expression on his face.

I wish I knew what he was thinking.

Before long, the others joined us, Alexi and Verity curling up on a love seat. Logan sitting beside his mate, his arm wrapping around her as his hand rested on the small bump now beginning to show.

"So, how did shopping go? Did you manage to get

everything to decorate the nursery?" Verity asked, once we were all settled.

"Yes, everything on the list anyway. The rest we can get at the baby shower, my mother has created some crazy gifting list." Andy chuckled, Alexi and Logan joining her.

"It's mum, I'd expect nothing less." Alexi said, still chuckling.

"When's the shower again?" Logan asked.

"Next month."

A smile spread over his face as his eyes went to Grayson.

"That's it! there's your answer."

Grayson's eyebrows furrowed as he stared at Logan.

"Answer to what?"

"Your mate, we can invite everyone from the engagement party. No masks this time, you'll see her face."

A hopeful look filled Grayson's eyes as he considered the idea.

"And if she doesn't show?"

"Then we'll know that she is whoever is missing."

"You're forgetting it's not for a month." Alexi spoke, making the two excited wolves quiet.

"You don't have to wait until the party, you can start looking now, right? Most of the guests were from the pack, you can try to find her here first. If you can't, then at least you'll know she'll be at the party." Verity offered.

The boys both nodded along as she spoke, eager to have a solution.

"Then it's settled. Let the mate hunt begin." Logan cheered.

## *Chapter 12*
Megan's POV

The next day went by in a blur of tedious tasks and demands by the former Luna, who apparently is in charge of planning the baby shower.
By the time my shift was finished I was exhausted and ready to collapse on my bed.
Walking out of the packhouse, I waited for my ride. My father always picked me up when he finished work early, I think he just likes the excuse to ask questions about my day. When you're stuck in a car there's nowhere to run to avoid answering him.
"Hey Megan wait up." Alexi yelled as I started to walk to the front entrance of the packhouse.
Stopping, I waited for him to catch up to me.
"Is everything okay?"
He nodded, slightly breathless as he stopped in front of me.
"Yeah fine, I'm asking everyone questions. Let me walk you out?"
With a nod, I started walking again, this time with Alexi beside me.
"So, you were at the party last week, right?"
I felt myself tense, as my heart began to race.

"Yeah, why?"

"I'm helping Grayson, trying to find out if anyone recognized her. or could describe her with any more detail."

"I was there with a friend of mine, but we left early. So, I didn't see anything."

I blurted, eager to end the conversation.

For a second, he didn't answer, and I started to worry I had been caught.

Eventually he nodded, smiling.

"Thanks anyway Megan, see you tomorrow."

"No problem." I said as he turned and ran back to the pack house.

Sighing I saw my father park up, rushing I got in the passenger side.

"How was work kiddo?"

"Boring."

He looked towards me, unconvinced.

"Who was the boy who walked you here?"

I rolled my eyes.

"The beta, Alexi."

"Is he a 'friend.'"

"No, his mate's a friend though, her name is Verity." I said, hoping he'd except that and leave the topic alone.

"I know you haven't found your mate yet sweetie, but he's probably closer than you think."

You have no idea.

"I know dad, I'm not worried."

With a nod, his gaze went back to the road, and we drove in silence the rest of the way.

By dinner, my exhaustion had lessened. A warm meal and comfy pajamas giving me a boost of energy.

Curling up on the couch, I grabbed the remote.

Turning to Netflix, to see what was on.

The front door swung open, Wes walking in.

"Honey I'm home." He yelled, causing my father to groan a little too dramatically to be real.

Laughing Wes came and joined me.

A rueful smile on his face as he eyed me.

"What did you do?" I groaned as he collapsed on the couch.

His hand went to his chest feigning insult before he laughed.

"I didn't do anything, I have gossip."

Groaning, I shifted so I was facing him.

I know him well enough to know there's no point arguing.

He is going to tell me if I want to hear it or not.

"Apparently, the alpha and beta are going through the pack, asking questions to every girl. Trying to find any information on Grayson's mate. Their talking about rounding everyone up at the packhouse, so he can meet them."

My heart began to race, my body tensing. They really are looking for me now, I can't keep this up forever.

"What am I going to do?" My voice came out as a whisper.

"I'm not sure Meg's, your hidden for now. But you can't wear that thing forever. And eventually you need to make a choice."

My head fell into my hands.

He's right.

Of course, he's right.

I need to reject Grayson.

# Chapter 13
Grayson's POV

Groaning, I collapsed on the couch in the tv room. Alexi and Logan have been going through the entire pack for days. Linking me as they talk to every she wolf they can find.

At first, I joined them, talking to them myself. But after two days of unmated she wolves throwing themselves at me, my wolf was becoming hard to control.

He wanted to kill them for touching us.

So here I am, hiding in the packhouse. Hoping they'll find something.

After a while of silence Alexi linked me.

*How are you doing Gray?*

*Great.* I drawled.

*Have you found anything?*

For a second, he didn't say anything, I was worried he had cut the link.

Until he finally responded.

*Not a lot, most people didn't notice her. and from what you told us and the few things we have been told. We can at least narrow down the list.*

*Narrow how?*

*We know she's young, maybe 18-25, black hair,*

*light brown skin. We're unsure about her height, we can assume she was wearing heels at the party, so under 5,5 I would guess. As for the guys she was with, no one knows who he is.*

A growl slipped through my lips at the mention of *him.*

*My guess theirs maybe fifteen girls who match that description in the pack.*

Fifteen...

I could feel Alexi's silence echo through me.

*What is it?*

With a sigh he replied.

*We haven't tried everyone yet, there's still one more possibility, we haven't considered.*

*Just say it.*

*The mated she wolves.*

A growl left my lips as I stood, the wooden table shattering as it collided with the wall.

*Mine.* My wolf growled.

My hands fisted as I tried to control myself.

The sound of someone gasping had me turning around.

Andy stood in the doorway, her eyes watching me worriedly.

"I'm sorry about the table."

Smiling Andy sat on the couch, patting the seat beside her.

"It can easily be replaced, what happened Grayson?"

My head fell into my hands, feeling defeated.

"Alexi said we need to try the mated she wolves as well."

Sighing she wrapped an arm around my shoulders, pulling me in to her.

"I doubt she's mated, she's young right? She probably got nervous and ran. You'll find her, or she'll find you. Trust me."

Nodding, I stayed like this for a while.

Enjoying the comfort.

Even my wolf accepted her touching us, she was our friend and our Luna.

Over the next few days, I was starting to feel slightly more hopeful.

Maybe Andy was right, maybe she just needed time.

Training had been uneventful, the warriors all keen to listen to their Luna.

Mostly because she knew what she was talking about, and they knew it.

And because all male wolves know one thing.

Never anger a pregnant she wolf. especially not an alpha.

Andy was definitely starting to notice the

pregnancy now.
Wolves had short pregnancies, only 5 months.
So, in human terms Andy looked and felt 5 months pregnant already.
Huffing, she stormed out of the training arena.
"You, okay?" I asked, trying to keep my voice light.
Her eyes glowed flame blue as they turned to me.
"I'm fine." She growled.
Taking a step back, I averted my gaze.
From the corner of my eye, I saw Alexi making his way towards us. A smile plastered on his face.
"Hey little sister, what?" Alexi stopped as she glared at him.
"You called me fat." Andy yelled.
Alexi paled, his eyes widening.
"No, I didn't call you fat. I just thought maybe…"
He trailed off, not wanting to complete his sentence.
"You just thought I was having TWINS!"
His eyes found mine, silently begging.
With a shake of my head, I stepped back.
I have no intension of getting in Andy's way…
Andy rounded on her brother, her eyes flaming as she stepped towards him.
"Andy, remember you love me. I'm your favorite."
He whimpered, stepping away from her. his hands raised in front of him as a shield.

"Run." She growled.

Alexi wasted no time, turning he ran towards the packhouse.

Her gaze turned, meeting mine.

With a sigh, she calmed. Her eyes returning to their natural blue.

"That'll teach him not to call me fat."

With a laugh, she linked her arm through mine, and we walked towards the packhouse.

Andy pulled me through the packhouse, before finally settling in the TV room.

"You're with me today, you're on guard duty."

Laughing, I sat beside her on the couch.

"What happened to your actual guard?"

She glared at me, huffing.

"I fired him, I don't need a guard, Logans just being overprotective. Apparently, rogues keep coming on our land."

"That seems like a good reason for a guard."

"I can protect myself." She growled.

"I know, but it doesn't hurt to be safe. There's two of you to guard now."

Sighing, she nodded. Her hand resting on her swollen belly.

"I know, that's why you're here. You're one of the few people I can tolerate at the moment."

A smile graced my lips as she spoke. A sense of pride filling me and my wolf.
She chose us, above everyone. She chose us to keep her safe.
"Then I accept the honor."
Smiling, she turned on the TV.

As Andy starts her third movie, I decide to excuse myself, my stomach growling.
As soon as I enter the kitchen, I head straight for the fridge.
Cheering as I spot Andy's chocolate cake.
She had spent all day yesterday baking. Everything from cookies to cakes. The chocolate fudge cake is by far my favorite.
Cutting myself a massive slice, I grab a fork.
As soon as the cake hits my mouth I moan.
Giggling pulls my attention and I turn to see Megan staring at me.
I can feel my cheeks heat as I swallow.
I hadn't even heard her come in.
"How long have you been standing there?"
"Long enough." She said smirking.
"I was hungry…"
"I could tell."
Still smiling she tore a sheet of kitchen paper, handing it to me.

"You have icing on your face."

Thanking her, I take the paper. Wiping my face quickly.

With a wave, she leaves the room, a box of cleaning supplies in her hands.

Shaking my head, I grab my plate and re-join Andy.

## *Chapter 14*
### Megan's POV

I had spent days avoiding Grayson.
Avoiding the inevitable.
I didn't want to reject him, I tried to find a way around it, but nothing was working.
So, when I walked into the kitchen and he was there, I froze.
My wolf whining, begging me to go to him.
Everything about him was better than I remembered. From his silk black hair to his mesmerizing grey storm eyes.
I was so distracted staring at him that when he started moaning, I couldn't stop the laugh that left my lips.
His eyes shot to mine as a light blush covered his cheeks.
Even embarrassed he looked hot.
How is that possibly fair?
I look like a burnt tomato when I blush…
"How long have you been standing there?" his voice came out shaky.
With a smirk, my eyes connected with his.
"Long enough."
"I was hungry." He defended.

"I could tell." I whispered as I noticed chocolate running down his cheek.

Suppressing the urge to lick it off, I handed him a paper towel.

"You have icing on your face."

He wiped his face, smiling gratefully at me.

Ignoring my begging wolf, I grabbed my supplies and left.

Wanting to put as much distance between us as I could.

*Mate.* my wolf growled.

No.

We need to stay away from him.

*Mate.* She growled again.

Blocking her I went back to work.

By the time I had finished cleaning the packhouse, I was exhausted.

With a sigh I packed away my supplies, jumping as a voice spoke out behind me.

"Hello Megan, have you finished work?"

Turning I spotted Verity standing in the doorway, her eyes studying me.

She smiled as I nodded.

"Good, I wanted to ask for your help. I'm trying to pick a gift for the baby shower, but I have no clue what she'd need or want."

Smiling, I walked up to her. Motioning for her to lead the way.

Verity led me up the winding staircase, until we reached the Beta's floor.

Without a word she turned to the right, entering one of the rooms.

The room screamed Alexi, from the stacks of DVD's to the wall sized flat screen.

With a small smile Verity sat on the bed, pulling her laptop on her lap.

"Thank you for doing this, I didn't know who to ask know who else to ask."

"It's fine, really, I don't mind. I still need to decide on a gift anyway."

Relaxing slightly, she turned her attention to the screen.

An hour later, we had both ordered our gifts.

With a quick goodbye to Verity, I left the packhouse.

The sun had already set, leaving just the half-moon to light my path.

I would be walking home tonight, Wes was busy, and my father is on patrol.

With a sigh, I began the grueling hike home.

It didn't take long for the darkness to take on an eerie silence.

No crickets, birds or any forms of wildlife daring to make a sound.

Goosebumps covered my skin as I pushed myself to walk faster.

The sound of leaves crunching beneath my feet echoed through the air.

The wind changed, as the scent of dried blood filled my nose I started to run.

Ignoring my aching legs as my muscles burned.

Rogues.

The crunching of twigs sounded behind me as they stopped treading carefully.

I has smelt them, and they know it. There's no point in hiding anymore.

As a rush of air hit me, I dropped by sheer instinct.

The rogue jumped over me, missing me by only an inch.

Pushing myself off the ground, I forced my legs to move.

Another rogue jumped, landing a few feet in front of me. Blocking my escape.

Snarling, he lunged for me, his teeth tore into my arm. Recoiling in pain, the skin tearing as I ripped my arm from his mouth.

Swinging my leg, it connected with his. Both of us crashed onto the ground. His head colliding with the dirt.

Bruised and bleeding, he laid there dazed.
Grabbing my injured arm, I pushed myself up and ran.
The first rogue lunged for me again, this time tackling me to the ground. A scream rips from my throat as his claws dig into my back.
Get up.
I need to get up.
His claws dig deeper, pressing me into the ground.
Come on, focus.
There has to be a way out, there's always a way out.
Howling echoed through the trees.
The rogue searched the dense woods, his weightlifting from me as he prepared to fight whoever was coming.
In the blink of an eye, a wolf burst from the tree line. Colliding with the rogue, knocking them both to the ground.
With a deafening crack the russet wolf snapped the rogues neck.
As the rogue landed on the ground in a heap, the russet wolfs eyes shot to mine.
Storm grey, glaring in the darkness.
Grayson.
"Megan?" my father's voice whispered out, as he rushed to me.

His eyes scanned over my wounds, cussing under his breath as he tried to stop the bleeding on my back.

His arms went underneath me as he lifted me up. A pained cry left my lips as he started running to the pack hospital.

"I'm sorry, hold on. We're almost there."

My vision blurred as he spoke, before I could respond, the darkness took me.

# Chapter 15
Megan's POV

The smell of antiseptic filled my nose, and I knew where I was, even before I opened my eyes. Slowly I let my eyes drift open, flinching at the sunlight shining through the window.
The monitor beside me beeped as I searched the small room. The beeping sped up as my eyes landed on Grayson.
He was sitting in one of the armchairs, his head leant against the back of it as he slept.
Why is he sleeping in here?
Panicked my hand flew to my neck, gripping the necklace.
If I'm still wearing it...
Unless he touched me.
The beeping grew louder as I panicked.
He knows I'm his mate.
Grayson's eyes darted open, in a flash he came over to me, his eyes searching me.
"What it is? does it hurt? I'll get the doctor."
"Stop, I'm fine."
Pausing, Grayson turned to me. He looked unconvinced as his eyes travelled over me again.
"What are you doing here Grayson?"

His eyes met mine, a slight blush coating his cheeks.

"You were hurt, your dad had to take Wes home. He was freaking out."

He smirked as he spoke, avoiding my gaze.

"I didn't want you to wake up alone, so I stayed."

He doesn't know.

He can't if he did, he would say something right?

"Thanks, for staying and for last night. I thought I was done for, for a second there." I whispered, my arms hugging my chest.

"You're welcome."

Settling back into the bed I fought a yawn as I rested my head back on the pillow.

My whole body felt weighed down.

"You should sleep, you still need to heal." Grayson said, sitting back down in the armchair.

Too exhausted to argue, I just shut my eyes and let myself drift off.

By the time I woke up again, the sun was setting.

Again, Grayson sat in the armchair. This time however he looked better, his clothes clean, hair washed and the darkness beneath his eyes has lightened.

Beside the bed sat a massive get well soon balloon bouquet.

Infront of it, a bunch of purple daisies sitting in a

pink vase.
Wes.
Picking a flower, I read the card propped against the vase.

Megs x

Please never do that again, my heart can't take it!

PS: Love you x even if you prefer weeds to actual roses.

Wes x

Smiling, I put the flower back, spotting another gift as I did.
Hidden behind the flowers laid a book, a big pink bow surrounding it.
As I grabbed it, I read the cover.
The Hobbit.
One of my favorites, smiling I opened the book, inside the first page sat a piece of torn paper.

Megan,

I'm not sure if you'll like this, but I always read Tolkien when I get stuck in the hospital bed.

Sorry about the scrap paper, I couldn't make myself to write on the pages.

Grayson x

Laughing, I sat up.
Flicking through the pages, admiring the illustrations scattered throughout the book.
"Do you like it? Maybe I should've gotten chocolates or something." Grayson said as he glared at Wes's flowers.
"I love it. The hobbit's one of my favorites. Though I've never seen this addition before."
Relaxing, Grayson brought his chair closer.
"It's an anniversary addition, they re-released it with new illustrations."
Nodding, my eyes stayed glued to the book.
"Thank you."
Shrugging, he leaned back in his chair.
"If it's only one of your favorites, what are the others?"
Thinking it over, I tried to think what my favorites would be.
"Anything by Phillip Pulman, Neil Gaimon and Robert Jordan of course. The wheel of time series is by far my favorite."
He nodded at my choices, thinking for a moment.

"Tolkien is my favorite, though Robert Jordan would be a close second. Anything by Brandon Sanderson as well."

"Oh, I forgot about him! Mistborn was amazing."

"It's definitely one of his better ones. What about JRR martin?"

"Nope, I mean I liked it, but he kept killing my favorite characters."

With a laugh Grayson shook his head.

"It's what he does."

"What can I say, I like a happy ending. Sue me."

Still laughing he started to argue, only to be interrupted by a knock on the door.

"Come in."

Slowly, the door opened, my dad walking in.

A pile of boxes in his hands.

Wes followed close behind, a bag of what smelt like Tai food in his hands.

"Hey, you're awake!" Wes all but screamed as he rushed to me.

Pulling me into a tight hug.

Ignoring the pain shooting up my back and arm, I hugged him back.

"We brought supplies."

"I can tell."

My stomach growled at just the smell of the food, grabbing a container I dug in. Eager to calm my

## The Warrior's Daughter

growing hunger.

A moan slipped through my lips as I took a bite.

"This is amazing, I didn't realize how hungry I was."

Grabbing one of the containers my dad handed it to Grayson. Tilting his head, he looked up at my dad.

"You don't have to, it's fine. I can leave you all to eat."

My dad shook his head, handing it to him again.

"You saved my daughter's life, buying you dinner is the least I can do."

Thanking him, Grayson took the food. Joining us as we all ate.

Wes had climbed on the bed, his legs brushing against mine as we tried to fit on the small bed. Once we had all finished, my dad cleared up the leftovers. Before grabbing one of the boxes, they had brought.

"What exactly did you bring?"

As he pulled out another box a laugh slipped through my lips.

"Trivial pursuit? Really?"

"Yes, lord of the rings and normal. So, the rest of us stand a chance."

Pulling the table over my bed, he set up the game, his eyes going to Wes.

"There are chairs, you know?"

With a wink Wes simply replied.
"I know."
Groaning my dad handed us all our pieces, giving me Frodo, because I am always Frodo. To took Gandalf, Wes took Gollum. Grabbing the last piece my dad handed it to Grayson.
Who stared at the little plastic Aragorn figure confused?
"If you haven't read the books, there are questions on the movies too." Wes said.
"You'll lose either way, no one ever beats my daughter."

An hour later, my father and Wes were both intently watching, waiting for Grayson's answer.
He only needed one more correct answer and he'd win the game.
As soon as they realized, I might have finally met my match, the two of them had gotten a lot more interested in the game.
Smirking Grayson confidently stated.
"Friend. Mellon is elvish for friend."
A growl slipped through my lips as I nodded.
All three of them jumped to their feet, cheering.
Boys...
With a roll of my eyes, I started packing the game away.

"I can't believe you beat Megan; you have to come to our game nights from now on."

With a smile, Grayson's eyes drifted to me.

Dropping to the floor as they connected with mine. His cheeks darkening ever so slightly, I almost missed it.

Wes's eyes caught mine, his eyebrows furrowing as he bit his lip.

*I'm sorry Megs, I didn't think.*

Realization dawned on me, and I looked away from the both of them. Unwilling to show just how disappointed I truly am.

We can't do this again once I reject him. He'll want nothing to do with me, and the truth is I won't blame him. If it hating me makes it easier for him, then I'm willing to take all the blame.

The room fell into a tense silence causing my father to clear his throat.

"You should be resting sweetie, we'll be back in the morning."

With a kiss to my forehead, he ushered the others out of the room. Closing the door behind them.

Sighing, I closed my eyes. Willing sleep to take me.

## *Chapter 16*
Megan's POV

Once the doctors had finally released me, my dad drove me home, unwilling to let me walk after the other night.
I couldn't blame him; I wasn't particularly keen on walking home either. Every shadow, had me on edge as I scanned the tree line.
"So, that Grayson kid seems nice. Is he a *friend* of yours?"
Keeping my eyes trained out the window, I ignored him.
As the silence dragged on, I sighed, knowing that he wouldn't accept no for an answer.
"He's a friend, just a friend dad. Nothing more."
He can never be anything more.
The rest of the journey went by in silence, thankfully he didn't probe anymore out of me.
It was hard to lie to him, it's always been just the two of us. I've never kept anything from him before, and I couldn't be the one to tell him what she did.
Keeping up this lie with everyone was exhausting, so much more so than I thought it would be.

Because of one stupid, selfish decision everything has become so screwed up.

Grayson was in pain because of me, the only reason I've been doing any of this was to avoid him getting hurt.

Yet here I am, causing him pain anyway.

How did I let this all get so messed up?

If I had had the strength to reject him the moment we met, we wouldn't be in this situation. I wouldn't have spent all this time with him, wouldn't know him like I do now.

It would have been easier to stay away from him, but now…

Now, I know him.

I know the sweet guy who doesn't realize what he's worth. The guy who will put his life on the line to protect a virtual stranger.

The guy who's managed to make me like him, no matter how hard I try not to.

After two days of strict bed rest, I felt like climbing the walls. The room somehow feeling smaller than it ever has before. I need to get out of this room, to breathe fresh air again.

My wolf was restless, it's been weeks since I've shifted and she's beginning to fight me for her freedom.

Ignoring the ache in my back I walked towards the tree line, piling my clothes on a branch before shifting.

Fading into the back of my mind, I watched as my wolf roamed the trees, eager to explore after weeks of being locked away.

As the wind shifted and the scent of oranges filled my nose, I realized the mistake I had made by giving her complete control.

In a flash she was running towards the scent, eager to reach him. fighting against me as I struggled for control.

Putting everything I had to try to force her to stop before she did something I couldn't take back.

Grayson's eyes shot to us as we burst out of the trees. His eyes widening as they took in the scene in front of him.

For a brief second, he looked relieved, walking towards us, his hand outstretched.

My wolf rested her head against his palm, purring incessantly.

Her distraction was just what I needed to take back control of my body.

Slowly I backed away from his touch, regretting my choice as pain flashed in his eyes.

"Please, stay."

With a shake of my head, I continued backing into

the trees. My eyes never leaving his.

"Whatever is making you so afraid of me, I swear I'm not going to hurt you." He pleaded, stepping towards me slowly.

Pausing, I tried to explain myself with just a look. Not willing to risk mind-linking. We had spent too much time together for him not to recognize my voice.

If it weren't for the necklace, he would recognize my scent, but thankfully he had never seen me without it.

"Just one chance and I promise, I can prove to you that we could be happy together."

A whine slipped through my lips as he begged me. Carefully he stepped towards me, his hand outstretched again.

For a moment I allowed myself to be completely selfish and let him comfort me.

Knowing I'll regret it later. But right now, I needed him, needed the feel of his fingers brushing against my skin.

All the stress melted away, leaving me feeling two tons lighter.

"All you have to do is shift back and we can talk about this."

Tensing I moved away from him, ignoring the urge to do as he says.

With a shake of my head, I turn and run into the trees.

Grayson's yelling faded as I ran, until eventually, the air was silent.

Still, I circled the trees a few times, before heading home.

At least he won't be able to find my trail.

## *Chapter 17*
Megan's POV

Thankfully, the doctor cleared me to work after a couple more days at home.
Strangely, I was excited to do something, even if it was going to work.
As I entered the packhouse, Andy rushed for me, her arms wrapping around me.
"I heard you were coming back today; I've missed you. How are you feeling?"
Hugging her back I couldn't help but laugh as her bump pressed into my stomach.
I'd only been gone for a week, but her belly had completely swollen.
"I missed you too, and I'm all healed. How are you?" I asked, gesturing to her bump.
With a smile, she rested her hand on her stomach.
"We're okay, exhausted but okay."
Linking her arm with mine she pulled me upstairs.
"You're with me today. I'm desperate for the help."

Andy laid out a dozen colour samples, comparing each one.
All morning we had been setting up the nursery.

The crib, changing table and wardrobe were all done, and the room was beginning to come together.

However, Andy had yet to decide on a paint colour.

"I can't decide between the forest and the new hope." Andy mused; her eyebrows furrowed as she stared at the colors.

"How is new hope a colour? That doesn't even make sense." Alexi whined, as he lent against the wall paint brush in hand.

Andy had forced him to help as he was 'uncle' Alexi.

"They just give them weird names, it's basically just green or grey."

"Then why not just say green and grey?"

Shrugging I looked over at Andy as she glared at the samples.

"Screw it."

Spinning, she held up the new hope sample triumphantly.

Alexi cheered, picking up the grey paint and started on the walls.

By the time, the nursery was done, all of us were exhausted.

Collapsing on the couches in the tv room.

I slouched on the long corner couch, across from

Alexi and Andy. Colorful children's drawings hung on the walls, the pack children's artwork. This room was mostly used as a communal area, that all the pack were welcome to use, and the pups loved having their art displayed.

Andy had taken the pricey paintings of the wall after she became Luna, telling every pup their work could go up.

If I ever needed proof of just how selfless and kind she is, the dozens of crayon drawings will definitely do.

My muscles ached as I sat up, my body feeling over worked.

Why did I leave my bed again?

I whispered, unable to gather the energy to talk any louder.

"So, What now?"

Alexi groaned; his eyes tightly shut. "How about nothing? I can barely move my arms. I vote we have a group nap."

With a laugh Andy slowly nodded, whispering. "Agreed."

A nap did feel good, I felt as though I could easily sleep for a week. But one thing kept me from sleeping, my stomach growled loudly, echoing in the silence.

"I'm in for a nap, but I'm starving."

Instantly Andy perked up, her eyes opening as she turned to me.

"Food, we need food."

My eyes went to the door, considering just how far I would have to go to make it to the kitchen before even starting to cook something. Sighing, I turned back to the others.

"I won't make it that far, how exactly are we going to get food?"

The two of them shared a look before yelling out.

"Logan."

The three of us watched the door, waiting.

It didn't take long before Logan ran through the door, his eyes frantic as they searched the room.

"What is it? Is the baby coming? Crap, I'll get the towels." As he turned to leave Andy rolled her eyes. Whispering to me. "Men are idiots. What does he think he's going to do with a towel?"

Laughing, I shrugged.

Andy turned to her mate; her bottom lip pushed out as she looked up at him.

"The baby's fine handsome, their just hungry and we're all really tired from having to decorate the nursery without you."

Logan shuffled on his feet, his hand running through his hair.

"I'm sorry Little one, I had to work. How about I get

us Chinese? It's your favorite."

Andy nodded, keeping her eyes on the ground as she spoke. "I guess that would be alright."

"Perfect, I'll get it now. I won't be long."

Grinning Logan walked over to her, planting a kiss on her cheek before walking out the door.

Once he had left, I turned to Andy. She was back to sitting normally, a triumphant smile on her face.

"You're a genius." I said, impressed. She had acted that out flawlessly, even falling me.

The three of us were still laid across the couches when Logan came back. Bags of food in his hands as he sat beside Andy.

Dishing out the boxes, he handed each of us one before grabbing one for himself. From the amount of food laid out in front of us, I wouldn't be surprised if he cleared out the restaurant.

With a smile Andy kissed his cheek, careful of the bump on her stomach.

"Thank you, handsome."

A triumphant smile covered Logan's face as he grabbed a set of chop sticks and dug in.

All of us ate in a comfortable silence, no need to talk.

Just enjoying each other's company.

Eventually Verity joined us, sitting beside Alexi, her

head resting on his shoulders as he fed her one of his spring rolls.

She giggled as he pretended to offer her another, snatching it away and eating it at the last second.

The two of them were definitely well suited.

Verity had spent so long being miserable that Alexi's goofy, childish humour was what she needed.

I've never seen a frown on her face whilst he's around.

That's what a mate is supposed to be, someone who makes your life so much better.

My heart ached as I realized, I was doing the opposite to Grayson. He deserves so much more than I can ever give him. All I can do is bring my mate pain.

The others all waved as I left the packhouse, stepping outside into the sunlight. I felt myself relax as the warm light touched my skin.

The last images of summer floating away as the leaves fell from the trees. Crunching beneath my feet as I walked down the path.

Growling echoed around me, my sense of calm dissipating.

My heart raced as I searched the trees, praying I had imagined it. That it isn't happening again.

Silently I cursed myself for not asking Andy to join training. To at least learn how to defend myself rather than relying on someone saving me again.
A figure walked out of the trees, further down the path. Squinting, I tried to make them out. the sunlight silhouetted around them as they walked towards me.

Turning, I ran. Leaves crunching as I rushed over them.

My heartbeat filled my ears, drowning everything else out.

The packhouse came into view and I pushed my legs to go faster.

My feet hit the bottom step as a voice filled my ears.

"Megan!"

Stopping, I stayed on the steps to the packhouse. My eyes going behind me.

Grayson stopped; his breathing frantic from chasing me. His hair was disheveled, his eyes wide as he tried to catch his breath.

"I'm sorry, I didn't mean to scare you."

My hand rested on my chest as I tried to calm my speeding heart. it felt like it could burst from my chest at any moment.

"What made you growl? Was there a rogue?"

Shuffling on his feet, he avoided my eyes.

"No, there wasn't a rogue. I was fighting with my wolf; he's getting harder to control."

His eyes stayed on the floor, refusing to look at me. with a sigh, I sat on the step. The stone cold against my bare legs.

My voice came out as a whisper.

"Because of your mate."

Grayson nodded, sitting beside me. His arms resting on his knees as he looked towards the sun beginning to set between the trees.

My arms wrapped around my knees, pulling them to my chest.

For a while we both stayed like that, watching the sun go down as we ignore the issue he was faced with because it was an issue.

When a wolf has a mate bond they don't just want to be with their mate.

They need to be.

If they are kept apart, the wolves get aggressive and eventually with enough time can go feral.

My wolf wasn't feeling the effects as much because we were around him so much.

But Grayson's wolf can't feel us, so he's been denied his mate this whole time.

This is the whole reason rejection exists. Because it breaks the mate bond permanently, the wolves no longer need each other.

Meaning they can be apart and move on, allowing them to find another mate.

Eventually Grayson broke the silence as he whispered.

"I don't know what to do, I'm struggling to keep him in. He's only leaving me alone now because he likes you."

"I'm sorry."

"It's not your fault. I just wish I could talk to her, to explain to her that whatever it is that she's afraid of, I'll try to understand, try to help. But I can't, I don't even know her name."

My heart ached as he spoke, he sounds so defeated it's killing me.

Before I could speak, he keeps talking, his voice rising with his anger.

"Alexi and Logan have been searching for her, but they can't find anything. How is that even possible? I know she's in this pack, I saw her. how the hell can't they find her."

Standing up, he paced the path. His hands fisted at his sides as he tried to calm himself.

"I'm sorry, I shouldn't be yelling at you. This isn't your problem, its mine."

Forcing a smile, I tried to reassure him and myself that I'm okay.

"Its fine, I understand. Being apart from your

mate's hard."

His eyes found mine, tilting his head.

"You sound like you're speaking from experience."

"Not my own, my mother left my father after I was born. He doesn't talk about it a lot, but I know that she didn't reject him when she left."

His eyes widened as he sat beside me.

"I've seen him, his wolf isn't wild. How did he do it?"

Shrugging, I looked away from his gaze. Unable to watch the hope leave his eyes.

"I'm not sure, he doesn't talk about her. honestly, the only reason I know all of that is because I found her diary."

"I'm sorry, that must be hard."

His eyes softened as they found mine. Betraying his pity with just a look.

Before I could speak, Alexi's voice interrupted us.

"Hey Gray. I've been looking for you everywhere. Oh, hi Megan, I didn't see you there. Sorry I didn't mean to interrupt."

Standing, I brushed the dirt from my legs. Smiling as I turned to Alexi, he was standing above us, looking guilty.

"It's fine, I should be going now anyway."

For a second Grayson looked like he was going to stop me, but his eyes shifted to Alexi before finding mine again.

"Goodbye, Megan."

With a wave, I left them to talk. Finally heading home.

## Chapter 18
Megan's POV

By the next morning, I had replayed our conversation over in my head a hundred times. Grayson's struggling, his wolf is getting aggressive. Whether I want to or not, I need to reject him before the damage I'm doing can't be undone.
I made my way through the packhouse, cleaning the communal areas as I went.
As soon as I reached the alphas floor, I knocked at their bedroom door.
Almost instantly Andy's voice filled my ears.
"Come in."
She sat on her bed; her legs crossed with a book resting on her knee. A smile filled her face as I stepped into the room.
Her smile faltered slightly as she got a good look at me, her eyebrows furrowing.
"What happened?"
With a shake of my head, I motioned to the ensuite, cleaning supplies in my hand.
"Forget about that, somethings obviously bothering you."
She tapped the bed beside her, before discarding

her book. Her focus entirely on me as I sat beside her.

"Grayson's wolf is starting to go wild."

Her face paled as I poke, her shoulders slumping slightly.

"You know he's a good guy, whatever it is that has you holding back. He'll help."

With a sigh, I rested my head on the wooden headboard. My eyes closed as I whispered.

"It's not that easy."

"Try me."

"My mother's not a wolf, when she met my father, she didn't know he was her mate. she fell for him and got pregnant, but when he explained what he was, what they were to each other. She freaked. She was furious that fate decided her future for her. that her feelings weren't hers, they were because of the mate bond. So, she tried to destroy it, as if it never existed."

Andy's eyes widened; her head tilted.

"How could she do that?"

"She's a witch, something my father didn't know. But it was too late, the mate bond had been formed. There was no way to destroy it completely. Rejection would help wolves, but the human side would still feel the effects of the bond."

"So, she didn't break it?"

"You don't understand."

"When my mother realized her mistake, she decided to correct it with me. She couldn't destroy the mate bond with my father because it had already been set."

"So, she gave me a parting *gift*."

"She cursed me. She wanted to make sure if I ever met my mate that it couldn't chain me, like it did her."

"What does that mean?"

"It means that if the bond is completed it will kill him."

Andy watched me, stunned. Her mouth hung open as she thought through my words.

"She did that to you. Can't you ask her to undo it?"

With a shake of my head, I fought a sob as I said. "She left afterwards; we haven't seen her since."

Tears dell from my eyes as my body shook. Andy's arm went around me, pulling me towards her as her hand stroked my back.

"I didn't know what she did, until a few months ago. I found her journal, she wrote everything down, including the spell she used in me. And this." I gestured to the gem hanging around my neck. "She used it to keep herself separate from my dad, so he couldn't find her. it conceals the bond. I can feel it, but Grayson can't. Not unless he touches me."

Her arms stayed wrapped around me as I broke down, everything I had been holding back, exploding out at once.

My mother did this to me, because of her I can never have a mate because of her I can never have Grayson.

## *Chapter 19*
### Megan's POV

"Megan, hurry up or we'll be late." Wes shouted. Rolling my eyes, I squeezed into the baby blue dress he had forced me to wear.

Today was Andy's baby shower.

After my break down with Andy, I had decided to wait until after her shower to talk to Grayson. It wasn't fair to her to ruin it, especially after everything she's done for me.

Wes had agreed to be my `Date` so that I could stay with him and avoid Grayson, and the others.

Alexi and Logan were on the hunt for his mate, they had invited everyone from the engagement party. Meaning they were going to be extra vigilant today.

I needed to stay off of their radar, at least until I talked to Grayson. He deserved to hear it from me.

As I walked down the stairs, Wes shook his head. His foot tapping the floor as he glared at me.

"Took you long enough."

Sticking my tongue out I left the house, letting the door close behind me. Smirking as a pain whine sounded from inside.

The door had hit Wes as he turned to leave.
His hand rubbing the red patch on his forehead, he glared at me.
"You so did that on purpose."
"I don't know what you mean."
Glaring, Wes jumped in the truck.
Starting it as I joined him.


The packhouse had been completely decorated in pink and blue for the party. No one knew if the new alpha was a boy or girl and Andy's mother had decided on a gender reveal today.
Andy wasn't keen on the idea of waiting to find out but when her mother explained they were using a cake Andy agreed.
The promise of cake all she needed.
Even the guest had to wear pink or blue. Wes being Wes was wearing a bright pink suit.
The garden had been set up for the party, tables covered in Buffett food lined the edges. Leaving a massive clearing filled with tables and chairs.
The few male wolves who had been invited all wore dark blue suits, Wes the only one willing to wear pink.
Well truthfully, more than willing...
Wes straightened his back, proudly moving through the crowd. His eyes searching.

All of a sudden, he pulls us around the crowd. As Andy and Logan came into view, I realized who he was looking for.

"You look amazing, I told you it would suit you." With a smile Andy pulled him in for a hug.

"Thank you, I love it."

As Andy released Wes, Logan wrapped an arm around her. Pulling her back towards him. Giggling, she leant her head against his chest. Grayson waved to us, making his way through the crowd. With a wave, I pulled Wes away. Hiding in the crowd, just in time to miss him.

"You know, we don't actually have to hide from him. I mean wouldn't that be more suspicious?" Wes whispered as we broke out of the crowd, his hands on his hips as he glared at me.

"Shut it."

With a roll of his eyes, he turned to the buffet table beside us. Filling a plate.

As the party carried on, my efforts to avoid Grayson had proved effective. I hadn't seen him all day.

Andy and Logan both stood at the largest table, a massive intricate cake in front of them.

The crowd gathered around, all eager to see if it's a boy or girl.

Beside me, a short older woman watched on, a

smile on her face.

Her black curls tied up, out of her face.

As I stopped beside her, she turned to me, her smile growing.

"What do you think, boy or girl?"

Her head tilted as she waited patiently for my answer.

"I'm not sure. Maybe a girl? I think Logan's hoping for a girl."

Her eyes widened at my comment. Anyone who's not high ranking would never call the Alpha by his name like that.

But I'd spent so much time with them now that I had gotten used to referring to them by their names.

The woman's smile returned as she looked over me.

"You must be friends with Andrea?"

This time it was my turn to be surprised.

I'd never heard anyone aside from her parents refer to her as Andrea.

"Yes, how did you know?"

"Because she has good taste. Though I suppose I am biased, she's friends with my son."

With her finger, she gestured to the two men beside Andy.

"He's the one on the left, he thinks it will be a girl

also."

My stomach dropped as I realized who she's referring to.

As I look at her, their similarities are obvious. The jet-black hair, grey eyes and kind smile made her the spitting image of Grayson.

Unaware of my anxiousness, she continued smiling as we waited for Andy and Logan to cut the cake.

Ignoring the growing pit in my stomach I watched the happy couple as they pulled out a pink slice of cake.

Grayson and Alexi both cheered. The crowd roared, cheers and congratulations being shouted at the celebrating couple.

Slowly the crowd began to disperse, going back to their conversations.

Grayson's mother turned to me; her hand outstretched.

"My name is Tara."

"Megan." I replied shaking her hand.

"Hey, mum. I told you it'd be a girl."

Grayson said running up to us, pausing as his eyes found me.

"Hey, Megan. I didn't see you there."

Tara's eyes shifted between us, her eyebrows furrowing.

Eyeing the two of us, she embraced Grayson.

"I'll leave you two alone. It was a pleasure to meet you, Megan." She said as she turned to leave.
Grayson watched her leave, a small smile on his face.
"I haven't seen her smile like that in a long time."
He must have noticed my confusion because he explained.
"My father died a couple of years ago. She took it hard, hasn't left the house since. Andy visits her, she wanted to return the favor."
"I'm sorry about your father."
With a smile that didn't quite reach his eyes, he shrugged.
"It's okay, happened a while ago."
Unconvinced I dropped the topic, something telling me he didn't want to talk about it.
"Do you want to go for a walk?"
Tensing, my eyes searched for Wes. Biting my lip when I came up short.
Noticing my hesitation, Grayson stepped closer to me, his eyes connecting with mine.
"Please, I just want to talk."
Slowly, I nodded.
With a grin, he led me away from the crowd. Behind the house, towards the beach. As we descended the stone stairs built into the side of the cliff, he finally broke the tense silence.

"I, wanted to talk to you about something."
His eyes dropped to the ground, shuffling on his feet, nervously.
"Talk to me about what?"
"You being my mate."

## *Chapter 20*
Megan's POV

How did he figure it out?

My heart raced as he stared at me, my breathing stopped as I tried to calm my heart.

"What? What are you talking about?"

"My wolf needs a mate; without a rejection he's breaking. The only way around it is to create a bond with another wolf. he likes you, and so do I. I wanted to ask if you'll be my chosen mate."

He wants me to be his mate, to replace his fated mate.

Me.

Ignoring my wolfs howl of joy that he choose us. Without the bond, without fate forcing him to.

*He still wants us.* She finished my thought.

He's also giving up on us.

He's replacing his mate, remember?

With a growl she put up her wall.

Tears welled in my eyes as he watched me, waiting.

"I... I can't."

His face fell.

"I know it's a lot to ask, but I've never felt like this before. I can't get you out of my head. The way you talk with so much passion about Tolkien, the way your face lights up any room you're in."

Taking a step towards me, his hand reaches out towards my face.

Before it can connect with me, I flinch. Backing away up the stairs.

"We can't. I'm sorry."

"Why? I know you feel something for me. I can see it in your eyes, every time I catch you staring. Please, just give it a chance. Just a chance."

Shaking my head, I whispered through a sob.

"I'm sorry. I can't."

Avoiding his gaze, I turned and ran up the stairs, ignoring his shouts as I ran.

As my foot reached out for the top step, it slipped causing me to stumble and fall back.

My back collided with something solid, preventing me from fall the full height of the cliff.

As sparks spread over my skin, I froze.

Strong hands gripped my arms, holding me upright.

In a flash I jumped back, out of his reach.

It was too late though, if I had felt the sparks, then so had he.

My secret was out.

After months of hiding, of being too afraid to tell him the truth.

Too selfish to reject him, like I should have from

the beginning.

As I forced myself to look up, my heart raced. Expecting to find Grayson furious after everything I've put him through.

But instead, he just looked…

Hurt.

"I… I don't understand."

He whispered, his eyes travelling over me. as if he were searching for answers.

"I, I'm sorry."

His eyes met mine, the grey storm making my heart ache.

"This whole time, you've been right in front of me. I thought you were afraid of me, but you're not. You just don't want to be mated to me."

As he spoke, his voice grew louder, angrier. His gaze on me hardened.

"No, I…"

Wes's voice interrupted me, and our eyes flew to the top of the steps.

Wes stood, his eyes shifting between the two of us as he moved towards us.

Grayson tensed, a small growl leaving his lips as he glared at Wes.

"You just chose him." he sneered as Wes's hand rested on my shoulder, trying in vain to offer me some comfort.

With a shake of my head, I began to explain only to stop myself.
He deserved to hate me.
To blame me.
It would be easier for him than the agony I feel knowing the truth. Every time I look at him knowing he wants me, but we can never be together, that despite fate we can never be mates. Can never be anything to each other. Or worse, what if he sides with Wes, that maybe there's a chance everything will be okay. There's no way I'm risking his life on a maybe.
So, finally deciding to put him first, I didn't say anything.
Instead, I moved closer to Wes, avoiding Grayson's gaze.
As a growl filled the air, he pushed past us. Is shoulder brushing mine as he rushed up the steps.
"Fine, you get your wish."
Sobs wrecked my body as Wes's arms wrapped around me.
My head rested against his chest, taking comfort in his warmth.
After a while staying like that, just holding each other in silence. Wes finally spoke.
"Why did you let him believe I'm the reason? He's going to hate you and none of this is your fault."

"Isn't it? I wasn't strong enough to tell him from the beginning, I dragged it out and put him through so much pain."

As Wes tried to interrupt, I put my hand up stopping him.

"Besides, blaming me will be easier for him. he can move on, find someone worthy of him."

Wes's eyes softened as I spoke, his grip on me tightening.

"If this is what you want, then I won't argue with you. But you need to understand that you are worthy enough. And you do not deserve any of the blame."

With a weak nod, I squeezed my best friend. Placing a quick kiss on his cheek before releasing him.

"Let's go home." He said, linking his arm through mine as we climbed up the steps.

Ignoring the crowd we made our way back to the truck, hopping in and speeding away.

As the party faded into the distance my adrenaline faded with it.

My shoulders slumping as I stared out of the window.

Watching the trees go by as my mind recounted the day.

Grayson knows.

He knows who I am now.

A weight lifted from my shoulders.

No more lying, no more hiding from my problems.

At least it was finally over.

As least, maybe we can start to move on now.

## *Chapter 21*
Grayson's POV

"Do you want to go for a walk?"
Tensing, she eyed the crowd as if searching for an excuse to say no. Before she could find one, I stepped forward my eyes finding hers.
"Please, I just want to talk."
Slowly, she nodded.
As we walked behind the house, towards the beach. I led us towards the beach. As we descended the stone stairs built into the side of the cliff, I finally broke the tense silence.
"I, wanted to talk to you about something."
My nerves overwhelmed me as I tried to figure out the right words to say.
"Talk to me about what?"
"You being my mate."
Her eyes widened as she began to step away.
"What? What are you talking about?"
"My wolf needs a mate; without a rejection he's breaking. The only way around it is to create a bond with another wolf. he likes you, and so do I. I wanted to ask if you'll be my chosen mate."
Tears welled in her eyes as she whispered.

"I... I can't."
My heart ached; I had known that she might say no. Afterall it's not a small thing to ask of someone.
"I know it's a lot to ask, but I've never felt like this before. I can't get you out of my head. The way you talk with so much passion about Tolkien, the way your face lights up any room you're in."
Taking a step towards her, I reach a handout towards her face, trying to wipe a stray tear away. Before it can connect with her, she flinches.
Backing away up the stairs.
"We can't. I'm sorry."
"Why? I know you feel something for me. I can see it in your eyes, every time I catch you staring. Please, just give it a chance. Just a chance."
"I'm sorry. I can't."
Avoiding me she turned and ran up the stairs her foot slipping as she reached the top step.
Jumping up the steps I reached out just in time for her to collide with my chest.
As sparks spread over my skin, I froze.
Jumping out of my arms, she stepped away from.
How can this be possible, she can't be.
I can't feel the bond now, but I know I felt sparks. My wolf howled in agreement, he had felt them too.
"I... I don't understand."

I whispered, my eyes searching her.

"I, I'm sorry."

"This whole time, you've been right in front of me. I thought you were afraid of me, but you're not. You just don't want to be mated to me."

She never said anything, just let me think I'd never find my mate.

"No, I..."

As a Wes yelled down at us, she stopped.

"You just chose him." I sneered as Wes's hand rested on her shoulder.

I waited, praying she would deny it. Would tell me, she was just scared, and she wanted to be with me. But as she stayed silent and moved into his arms, I felt my heart shatter and my wolf break.

She choose him.

"Fine, you get your wish." I growled as I ran up the stairs.

I walked through the crowd, ignoring Alexi and Logan as they yelled for my attention.

I needed air, to get away from the crowd of people. Without a second thought, I turned and headed in to the packhouse.

As soon as I reached my room, I collapsed on my bed.

Megan's my mate.

This whole time she was right in front of me, and I

couldn't even tell.
How is that even possible?
How can I not feel the bond?
I still can't feel it.
If I hadn't of touched her, I'd never know.
She would've let me wolf go feral and done nothing to stop it.
My wolf whined, his pain seeping through me.
She was willing to let us lose ourselves and for what?
Some guy who isn't even her mate!
The walls shook as a growl left me, my anger taking over as I sat there replaying everything that's happened since I met my mate.
Every time I had seen Megan, had confided in her.
Every time I had trusted her.
Every time we had spoken, and she had lied to my face.

## *Chapter 22*
Megan's POV

Wes spent the night with his arms wrapped around me as we laid on the bed.
Never complaining.
Despite me soaking his shirt as I cried, he never said a word. Just held onto me, his hand rubbing my back until I eventually fell asleep.

The next morning, I woke to Wes's head resting on my shoulder as he unattractively drooled on my shoulder, still sound asleep.
With a sigh I maneuvered myself off the bed, making sure to be careful not to wake him.
As I stood, he groaned. Rolled over and went back to snoring as he drooled on my pillow.
After showering and changing out of yesterday's clothes I made my way downstairs.
The sound of metal banging against the hard floor had me rushing to the kitchen.
Standing in the middle of what appeared to be a war zone stood my father, red faced as he tried to brush flour off his shirt.
His eyes shot to me as I walked into the room, a frustrated sigh leaving his lips.

"Good morning kiddo, how are you feeling?"
Forcing a smile, I began cleaning up the kitchen, avoiding his eyes.
"I'm fine dad, what happened here? if you wanted breakfast, I would've cooked it for you."
With a sheepish look he shrugged.
"I was trying to make your favorite breakfast. You came home upset; I didn't realize how impossible pancakes are."
For a second, I just stared at my father in shock, he'd never cooked for me before. Something about him trying, even if it didn't go to plan, warmed my heart.
My father had never been particularly fatherly, he's a good dad, but he's been doing it alone from the beginning. He has to deal with his mate leaving in the middle of the night and leaving him with a two-day old baby.
As I grew, we developed a routine, I made breakfast, went to school and took care of myself and he would work and pick me up.
Even if I don't need a ride, he still takes me, and we do our catch up. Because in his own way he still wants to know about me and my day.
Except last night, he heard me crying and wanted to help in any way he could.
"Thank you, I'm okay."

As the words left my lips, he turned to me, his eyes softening.

"No, you're not. What happened? Please tell me, maybe I can help."

Sighing, I rested against the counter. My gaze fixed on the floor as I spoke.

"You can't, not with this. I promise dad, I will be okay."

He looked unconvinced as he went back to cleaning.

Thankfully, he didn't press the topic and it wasn't long before the mess was gone, and the smell of pancakes filled the air as they sizzled in the pan.

Eventually Wes's slumped form walked into the room, his eyes fixed on the stack of food.

We all sat and ate in a comfortable silence until my father excused himself to leave for work.

Leaving me and Wes alone.

As we packed away our plates Wes turned to me, biting his lip.

"I had an idea last night."

When he didn't continue, I turned to him expectantly.

"What if the curse wasn't there?"

"What do you mean not there? It's our mate bond that's cursed. Until we sever the bond, it will be there."

He shuffled nervously, avoiding my gaze before whispering.

"I found her."

It took me a second to realize who he was referring to.

"How?"

"I asked my dad."

Shocked I stared at my friend.

He never asks his dad for anything; they've barely said a word to each other in years.

But he's asked for his help.

For me.

"Thank you."

Relaxing, his lips spread into a smile.

"Where is she?"

"London."

My mothers in London, after all these years she's a few hours away.

"I've already put it in my sat nav, get dressed and we can go."

With a hug to Wes, I rushed upstairs, ready to change.

"Ready?" Wes asked as I bounded down the stairs.

"Yep, just need to tell Andy we are going. We were supposed to have lunch."

With a nod, he opened the door. Ushering me out as I sent Andy a text.

I'm going to meet my mother...

My excitement grew as we got closer, the outline of London's dense buildings just visible in the distance.
As we drove my phone buzzed with a reply from Andy.

A – Are you okay? Grayson told me what happened.

M – Honestly, I don't know. At least he knows now.

A – We can talk? Are you home?

M – No, we're in London.

A – London? When will you be back?

M – I'm not sure.

"I think we're here."
Putting my phone back in my pocket I looked out at the massive town house that we'd parked beside.
Here goes nothing.

## *Chapter 23*
### Grayson's POV

By the next day, my anger had begun to subside. My head clearing.
I've found my mate.
I'm being rejected by my mate...
With a sigh, I knocked on the Alpha's suite door. Andy's voice filling the air almost immediately.
"Come in."
Sitting across the bed with her back rested against the headboard. Andy's gaze lifted to me as I stepped inside, a smile covering her face.
"Hey, we missed you yesterday. What happened?"
With a sigh I collapsed on the bed beside her.
"I found her."
Her eyes widened as she turned to me, giving me all her attention as she waited for me to continue.
"At the party, I found her. This whole time she was right there in front of me."
Andy's hand rested on my arm, calming me slightly as my heart raced.
"I just don't understand how she could lie to me like that. For months, she lied to my face."
Her eyes softened as she wrapped an arm around

me, careful not to squish her swollen belly.

"I'm sure Megan had her reason's; you should talk to her."

My body tensed as I pulled away from her.

Her head tilted as she caught my glare.

"I never said her name."

Eyes widening, she opened her mouth to defend herself.

"You knew? And you didn't tell me."

Rushing off the bed I backed away from her.

"I'm sorry, I…"

"When? When did you know?"

Her eyes glistened as they fell to the floor. So quite I had to strain to hear her, she whispered.

"I never didn't know."

A growl ripped from me, shaking the walls, without another look at her I turned and left.

Running down the spiral staircase as she yelled after me.

"Grayson wait, let me explain."

Her footsteps echoed the hall as she rushed to keep up with me.

"Grayson please, stop."

Anger consumed me as I spun around and faced her.

"Explain what? How you've been lying to me this whole time?"

"I'm sorry, but I didn't have a choice."
Another growl leaves me, making her take a step back.
Before I can say anything growling fills the room and we both turb to find Logan and Alexi watching us.
Logan looking ready to kill as he moves towards me, teeth barred in a snarl. His eyes darkening as he moves closer.
Andy turns to him with a shake of her head he relaxes slightly, still moving to stand beside her.
"I'm sorry for lying, truly I am. But I didn't have a choice."
Trying to keep myself as calm as I could, still weary of Logan and Alexi's gaze I turned back to Andy.
"Yes, you did. I thought you were my friend; how could you not tell me?"
"I am your friend, and I'm hers. I'm also her Luna, or did you forget that? It's not my place to force anything on her she doesn't want. She was afraid and she asked for help, no matter how much you mean to me Grayson, I will not deny someone help because you want me too."
The last of my anger disappeared, she's right.
"You're right, but it doesn't make it any easier."
Sighing Andy stepped towards me, Logan eyeing her worriedly. Ignoring him she wrapped her arms

around me, holding me tightly as she whispered against my shoulder.

"I tried to get her to tell you, and she was going to. After the baby shower, she just didn't want to ruin the party."

Was she really going to tell me?

A small piece of my heart mended at that.

She was going to tell me; she wasn't going to leave me in the dark forever.

"It doesn't really matter now, she chose him."

Andy backed away, her eyebrows furrowed as she looked at me.

"What are you talking about?"

"Some brunette guy, he interrupted us. She chose him, that's why she's rejecting me."

"You mean Wes?"

When I shrugged, she continued.

"The guy from the club?"

Nodding, I watched as Logan came back to her side, his eyes black again.

"I thought you said he wasn't a problem. He growled.

"Because he's not, you saw him at the shower. Do you really doubt it?"

Logan paused before nodding, Alexi chuckling behind him.

"What's happening?"

All three of them turned to me. Andy rested her hand on my shoulder as she spoke.
"She didn't choose Wes, she couldn't have, because Wes is gay."
Gay...
He can't be, she said they were dating.
*No, she didn't, you did.* My wolf growled.
She didn't deny it though.
*Maybe you left before she could.*
Guilt filled me as the image of her tear-filled face filled my mind.
Had I been too harsh?
I ran off before she could explain.
What did I do?
"I thought..."
Andy's eyes softened as she hugged me.
"Talk to her, but this time let her explain."
Nodding, I hugged her back.
"But first, have a shower. You smell worse than Alexi."
I chuckled as Alexi yelled an offended.
"Hey."

## *Chapter 24*
Andy's POV

After Grayson went back to his room, the others went back to work.
Once I had waddled back to my room, I collapsed on to the bed. Taking a well-earned nap.
Who knew growing a human could be this exhausting.

I woke up a few hours later, looking over at my phone to find a text from Megan.

M – Hey, sorry to cancel but I can't make it today.

A – Are you okay? Grayson told me what happened.

M – Honestly, I don't know. At least he knows now.

A – We can talk? Are you home?

M – No, we're in London.

A – London? When will you be back?

M – I'm not sure.

A - London?

Why is she in London?
My text went unanswered, so I put my phone away, heading in search of food.

## *Chapter 25*

Grayson's POV

After I left the others, I followed Andy's advice. Showering and changing into fresh clothes.
As soon as I had finished I all but ran to my car, excited to see my mate again.
She isn't with him; she never ran to be with him. For a brief second, I allowed myself to feel hopeful. To imagine that maybe, just maybe I might get to be with my mate.
My hope only grew as I drove to her house, thankful Andy had given me the address after I yelled at her.
As much as I want to blame her, I can't. She was right, she's the Luna and has to think about everyone not just me.
She was protecting my mate; she was her friend when she needed one and for that I truly am grateful to her.
As I parked my car outside, I tried to calm myself. I need to talk to her, and this time not let my emotions rule the conversation.
My heart finally slowed as I knocked on the door, waiting for her to answer.

## The Warrior's Daughter

As the door opened, Megan's father came into view, his eyebrows furrowing as he saw me.
"Good afternoon beta, did you need something?"
"Afternoon, I was hoping to speak to Megan."
He relaxed slightly, moving aside.
"I'm afraid she's not here, she was going to the packhouse with the Luna today."
Andy?
Why would she not tell me Megan's at the packhouse.
*Is Megan with you?*
It didn't take long for her to respond.
*No, why?*
*I'm with her dad, he thinks she's with you.*
For a second, she didn't answer, and I started to worry she had cut the connection.
*She cancelled our lunch, said she had to go to London.*
London.
Why London.
"Is there a reason she'd go to London?"
Mr Clarkes face paled as I spoke, his eyes widening.
My heart began to race as I waited for him to respond.
Worry consuming me.
The fear in his eyes fueling my own.
"Mr Clarke?"

As his eyes cleared, he turned to me.

"Her mother, she lives in London.

So, she's visiting her mother, why is that such a bad thing?

He noticed my confusion and sighed.

"My mate left when Megan was a baby, I never told her the whole story I thought it would be better for her that way."

"What is it that you didn't tell her?"

"That her mother almost killed her.

## *Chapter 26*
Megan's POV

Wes led the way to the house, his hand wrapped around mine.

I'm finally going to meet my mother after all these years.

"What if she doesn't want to see me?"

Wes squeezed my hand before knocking on the door.

A few seconds later the door opened, a tall woman with long black hair that perfectly framed her chocolate skin stood in the doorway.

"Can I help you?"

Her perfect eyebrows arched as she stared down at us.

"Hi, I um. I'm."

"Well spit it out, I don't have all day."

"I'm your daughter."

Her eyes widened, focusing on me.

"Well then, you best come in."

Moving aside, she gestured for us to come in. Closing the door behind us.

She led us to a living room, sitting on a deep red chair, motioning to the couch opposite her.

Wes sat down, pulling me to sit beside him, his

gaze fixed on my mother.

Noticing my silence, Wes spoke for me.

"I apologize for the intrusion Mrs Clarke but..."

"Edgerton, not Clarke, we we're never married. But please call me Cordelia."

"Cordelia, we came to ask for your help."

Her eyebrow raised as she waited for him to continue.

I watched her as she sat, her leg crossed over the other, hands in her lap.

Everything about her was the opposite to me, from the graceful way she sat to the perfectly pressed elegant clothes.

Nothing about her was out of place.

How can this person be my mother?

"We need you to remove the curse."

Her eyes widened as they flew to me, something I couldn't put my finger on swimming in them.

With a wide unnerving smile, she leant forward, her arms crossed on her knees.

"Well then you've come to the right place."

My stomach knotted; she's going to help us.

I can have my mate again.

Hope filled me for the first time in months, there's a chance.

"Well then, let's get started."

Standing, she crossed the room, sorting through

the massive cupboards lining the walls.
Wes's eyes found mine, his eyebrow raised in question. With a shrug I turned back to my mother.
"What do I have to do?" I asked after a few minutes of tense silence.
Her hand gripped onto something purple as she turned towards us.
"Sleep."
Wes's eyes darted to me again worry filling them. Before we could question her strange response, she uttered one word and darkness consumed me.
"Samnum."

## Chapter 27
Megan's POV

As the sound of voices filled the air, I began to wake.
My head pounding as I tried to understand what had happened.
As the memory flooded back, I felt myself panic.
My arms refused to move, burning bands covered my wrists and legs holding me tight to the stone table.
Wolfsbane.
My mother's voice paused my panic.
"Stop worrying Demetri, I told you. They're sound asleep."
Stilling, I strained to hear their conversation.
"Are you sure about this? It cannot be undone."
"Good."
Their voices faded onto the distance as they left.
Leaving me alone.
I waited until I could no longer hear them at all before opening my eyes.
The room was completely made of stone, even the floors.
One look at the chains holding me to the table and I knew I had been right about the wolfsbane.

Groaning had me forcing my head to turn, to look for the noise.

On the wall beside me, Wes sat, his back leaning against the wall.

His wrists bound in the same chains mine were.

Slowly, his eyes opened, as they connected with mine, he straightened.

Struggling against the chains that bound him.

"Megs?"

"I'm okay, just stuck."

Again, he struggled against the chains, with a frustrated sigh he slumped back against the wall.

"What happened?"

"I don't know, she said something and then I woke up here."

With a nod, he looked around the room, taking everything in.

"Are we actually in a torture dungeon?"

Wes said shaking his head.

"Who even has a torture dungeon?"

"Apparently, my mother does."

His eyes softened as I spoke.

"I'm sorry Megs."

"It's not your fault."

"I'm the one who got the address and drove us here." He scoffed.

I struggled against the chains trying to get to my

friend, to stop him from blaming himself.

"And if you had known this would happen, you never would've brought me here. This isn't your fault, Wes."

He nodded, unconvinced but dropping the subject.

"What are we going to do?" he whispered.

I looked away, unable to see the fear in his eyes as I whispered.

"I don't know."

We both remained silent for a long time, neither of us wanting to admit the truth.

That we are stuck here, that no one knows where we are or that we need help.

As the door creaked open, footsteps echoed through the room.

Growing louder with every step.

As the footsteps got closer, I began to struggle against the chains. Trying to put as much distance between us as possible.

Freezing as hands grabbed my wrists.

"Let go of me."

"Feisty, I like fiery women."

I forced my eyes to open as his fingers trailed up my arm.

His buzz cut combined with the dark chocolate colour of his skin making the edges of his face appear sharper and more defined.

He was a smaller build to Wes, more lean and thin. Definitely human not wolf, wolves naturally have more muscle. The effort of shifting more than enough to grow a significant amount of muscle.

"Leave her alone."

The guy glared at Wes, before moving towards him. In a flash he raised a hand and collided his fist with Wes's face.

"Stop, don't hurt him."

Laughing he turned towards me ignoring Wes's slumped body.

"It's not me you should be worried about sweetheart."

"What is that supposed to mean?"

With a wink he let out an eerie laugh before leaving the room.

As soon as the door closed behind him, I turned my attention to Wes.

His head rested against the wall as he tried to wipe the blood off his face.

His efforts were useless, the chains preventing him from reaching his bloodied nose.

His eyes locked on mine, and he forced a smile.

"I'd like to see him try that without the wolfsbane."

I watched my friend as he tried to make a joke out of everything, like he always did. To try and make everyone else feel better, never caring about himself. And I felt so thankful that I've gotten to have him in my life this while time.

Tears fell from my eyes.

He's here because of me.

"Hey, don't cry. You know how much it freaks me out when girls cry."

Before I could comment, the sound of the door opening had us both freezing.

Footsteps grew louder until my mother stood at the foot of my table. Her eyes gleaming in the dimly lit room.

She's enjoying this.

She's enjoying watching us chained up and helpless as she plays with us.

"You're sick. Why are you doing this?"

A smile spread over her mouth as I spoke.

A shrill laugh leaving her lips.

"My dear, I'm saving you."

"From what?"

"Yourself."

## Chapter 28
Megan's POV

She moved around me in a circle, her eyes inspecting me from head to toe.
Almost like she was looking for something.
"What do you mean from myself?"
"You'll understand soon." She whispered, moving away from me towards the end of the room out of sight.
Wes turned his eyes on me so much emotion in his eyes. It was as if I could read every word he was thinking.
'This woman is insane, I love you Megs, I'm sorry.'
I forced a smile, trying my best to return the look he was giving me.
Our eyes shifted to my mother as she came back into view, a small black box in her hands.
Her creepy smile was back as she stood at my feet staring down at me.
"Don't worry, you probably won't die. I can say the same for the boy however."
I struggled against my chains as she glared at Wes with so much hate it terrified me.
As the door creaked open, her gaze softened.
"Demetri darling, just in time for the show."

Her eyebrows furrowed when she didn't get a reply.

The footsteps stopped, sending the room into a tense silence.

"Demetri?"

Again, only silence answered.

"Darling, you know how I hate it when you play games like this."

When she still didn't get an answer, she began to walk towards the door.

Only to let out a hiss as a growl echoed through the room.

"I don't remember letting you into my home."

"I let myself in, darling."

My eyes widened as I searched the shadows.

I know that voice.

"Dad?"

My mother scoffed, rolling her eyes.

"You shouldn't have come. I won't let you stop me this time Johnathan."

This time?

What is she talking about?

Slowly, my father emerged from the shadows. His face etched in fury as he glared at his mate.

"If you hurt her Cordelia, I swear you will not leave this room alive."

"Such empty threats, you have no power. You're

alone, a dog whose growl is bigger than his bite."
As my father growled, she laughed, shaking her head.

"So predictable, all brawn and no brains. You forget the mate bond has been severed now, there's nothing preventing me from killing you this time."

My father lunged towards her, stopping as she yelled.

"Ignis."

As soon as the word left her lips, a wall of fire ignited in front of my father, blocking his path. He paced around the flames, his eyes shifting between them and me.

My mother turned towards me, grabbing the small black box she had discarded when my father arrived.

Carefully, she lifted a shimmering red gemstone out of the box.

"Why are you doing this?"

"You'll understand someday that this is for the best."

For the best?

"How is chaining us up in a torture chamber for the best?"

"Torture chamber? Really, that's a tad dramatic, don't you think?"

Slowly, she placed the gemstones on my stomach,

both hands cupping it.

"Leave her alone." Wes snarled, fighting against his chains.

"She doesn't belong to you, dog. I'm doing this for her."

"What are you talking about?" I plead, trying to get as far away from her as I could.

All my trouble only buying me a couple of extra inches.

"I'm going to finish what I started 18 years ago, before I was so rudely interrupted."

My father snarled. "Because it was killing her, you were killing her."

With a shrug, my mother went back to work, placing black petals on the table surrounding me.

"It was too early, they hadn't separated yet, I had to wait until she was older. Until they became two separate beings."

"What are you talking about? I don't understand."

With a sigh her eyes fixed on the wall behind me.

"And who might you be?"

Forcing my head to follow her gaze, I try to see who's there.

But there's nothing.

No one, just shadows.

"Not very chatty, are you? Well, it's no matter, you can watch the show too."

Ignoring the snarl that answered her, she turned back to me.

"You said you don't understand, but you found my grimoire. Did you not read the whole thing?"

She sighed as I shook my head.

"Children, so eager to skip to the end of the story, that they miss the most important part."

She sighed again, moving back to the gemstone.

"I only ever wanted to correct my mistake. I wanted to remove your parasite."

My eyes widened.

Parasite?

What is she talking about?

"It's your fathers fault, his genes. You were never supposed to be like this. You were supposed to be powerful, elegant not some dog who fights before they think."

My wolf, she thinks my wolf is a parasite.

"But it didn't work, you were joined. Until you were old enough to separate, to have your own identities. There was no way to kill one without killing the other."

A snarl came from the shadows as she reached for the gemstone.

"I came up with a spell, one that would solve everything. Your dog would die, and you wouldn't, elegant really. All I'd have to do is a ritual and leave fate to do the rest. Once your mate found you, one bite and the spell would take effect. Your dog dies, the added bonus being that your mate dies too."

The curse, it wasn't about the mate bond. It was always about being a werewolf.

"This whole time, it was because I have a wolf?"

"That wolf dominates you; it prevents any other genes from surfacing. You can either be a dog or a witch, but never both."

My blood ran cold as she casually talked about killing a part of me and Grayson.

As if it were any normal conversation.

"You're insane, why did you do that to me? You cursed me."

Her eyes widened as they turned on me.

"You never told her?"

My father growled, unable to get through the flames.

"You're father stopped me, forced me to leave before I could finish what I started."

He stopped her.

He saved me.

My eyes flew to my father as he fought an impossible battle to try and reach me.

This whole time I hadn't seen it, seen how much he protects me.

"I was never cursed."

"No, my dear, but you will be."
Her eyes shifted to Wes, tightening into a glare.
"And you will no longer believe you have the right to own my daughter just because fate decided it."
As her arms raised, she whispered.
"Diminium."
A burst of intense light shot from her hands into the stone.
Her eyes unfocused, clouding over.
In a flash a figure jumped from the shadows, knocking her to the ground.
With a shriek they landed on the floor out of sight.
"You got the wrong guy."
My heart began to race as I tried to see them.
It can't be him, why is he here?
With a crack the fire faded, my father rushing to the fight.
In an instant my father had his mate in his arms, her head hanging limp over his shoulder.
The chains around my wrists loosened before falling off. Fingers brushing against my skin as they fought with the chains on my legs.
The sparks travelling across my skin confirming what I already knew.
"Grayson?"
The chains cracked and fell as he moved into my eyeline, the grey storm calming as his eyes met

mine.

"Hello, Angel."

My heart jumped at the nickname.

Gently, he wrapped his arms around me, lifting me up.

Slowly he put me on my feet but leaving an arm wrapped around me as if he wasn't willing to let me go.

"I'm fine, just hanging out." Wes drawled, a little too dramatically.

I left Grayson's arms and rushed to him. Kneeling down to remove his chains.

"Finally, I thought you'd forgotten about me." He whined; his bottom lip stuck out for emphasis.

"Come on kids, time to go home."

## *Chapter 29*
Megan's POV


Wes curled up on the couch beside me, a bowl of popcorn in his hands.
"I still don't understand why you let him leave."
With a sigh, I paused the movie and turned to my friend.
"I told you, I just needed time. After everything. My mother and everything she did and was going to do. I just needed time and he understood that."
Wes rolled his eyes, shoving a handful of popcorn in his mouth.
"Grayson agreed because he's too nice, but Meg's it's been weeks. Hasn't it been long enough?"
Maybe he's right, after we had gotten back from London, I had told Grayson I needed to be alone. Too much has happened for me to think clearly.
"I know, you're right. I've been putting it off."
"Why?"
"After everything I did, all the pain I put him through. What if he can't forgive me?"
Wes's eyes softened as he wrapped his arms around me.
"Are you kidding? I saw the look in his eyes, that loves you. He will forgive you because you were

protecting him."

My eyes filled with tears as I stood up.

"I need to talk to him, find out where he is."

"He's at Andy's party. Its Halloween remember?"

Is it really Halloween already?

I've been hiding in my house for way too long.

"The party at the packhouse? I have to go."

As I reached the door I stopped, a groan leaving my lips.

"It's a costume party, they won't let me in without one."

Wes laughed, shaking his head.

"There's a costume on your bed."

Hope filled me as I hugged him, pressing my lips to his cheek before rushing upstairs.

Wes left as I changed.

Once I had finished, I made my way downstairs to Wes's truck waiting outside.

He drove off as soon as I got inside the car, a smirk covering his face as he saw me.

"You so did this on purpose."

A laughed left his lips as I whined.

The bright blue dress pulled so tight on my chest I could barely take a breath.

"I just thought it would suite you."

"Of course, you did, because dressing me up as a

princess who ran from a ball is just so entertaining."
Another laugh left his lips as I pouted in my seat.
"Don't worry Cinderella, we'll get you to the ball on time."
"I hate you, who are you even supposed to be?"
Wes sighed.
"Ren McCormack."
"Who?"
"Seriously, you need to watch more movies."
Before I could argue, he pulled up outside the packhouse.
Getting out before coming round to open my door.
"My lady."
Lacing my arm through his I let him lead me into the pack house.
A sense of Déjà vu swarming me as I saw all of the people dancing. All in costumes, faces covered, hidden under masks.
Wes pulled me to the dance floor, twirling me around in circles through the crowd.
Only stopping when a voice sounded behind me.
"May I cut in?"
Smiling, Wes nodded, releasing my hand. With a wink he walked off the dance floor.
Grayson stood behind me, his white tunic perfectly hugging every muscle. His jet-black hair gelled back

making the features in his face more prominent. His hand reached out to rest on my waist as the other grabbed my hand and we began to sway.

A realization dawned on me, and I couldn't help but laugh.

With a raised eyebrow, Grayson stared down at me.

"What's so funny?"

"I just realized, who you're dressed as. Did Wes help you with the outfit?"

For a second, he thought about it before his eyes trailed over my dress.

"Andy got it for me, though I'm thinking she may have had help."

We both laughed as we swayed across the dance floor.

As the song came to an end, Grayson stepped away reluctantly letting go of my hand.

For a second, he looked like he was going to speak but with a sigh he turned to leave.

"Wait."

His eyes flashed with hope as he turned to look at me.

"I was going to get some air, if you want to join me."

A smile spread over his face as he nodded, following me out of the ballroom.

We walked through the Luna's garden in silence until we reached the edge of the cliff, and Grayson broke the silence.

"I know you need time and I understand, I do. A lot happened and you need to sort through it all. I promise I don't mind waiting and I'll leave you alone."

His fingers ran through his hair as he shuffled nervously.

"I just wanted to know, to ask..."

His sentence went unfinished as he stared out at the water.

Taking a deep breath I moved towards him, reaching out to grab his hand.

"I did a lot of things wrong, made a lot of mistakes. I wish I could take them back and start over. If I had known that my father had stopped her. That I was never cursed..."

His gaze bore holes into my skin as he listened.

"You thought she had succeeded?"

"Yes, I thought that if I met my mate, if I accepted my mate he would die."

Slowly Grayson moved closer to me, his fingers trailing across my cheek.

"If you had known that there wasn't a risk. Would you have run?" he whispered, so quiet I had to strain to hear him.

"No, I would've stayed. I always wanted a mate and…"
Before I could finish his lips crashed against mine. Sparks exploded through me as his lips moved against mine.
I could feel his heart beating against his chest as the kiss pulled me in deeper.
He's mine.
And I'm his.
Cheering pulled us from our own world, as we broke the kiss, we turned to find the others all celebrating.
Alexi and Verity were dramatically swooning along with Wes, Logan and Andy clapping and wolf whistling.
"Finally." Andy said with a smile, her eyes shifted to Wes.
"One left."
With a shrug Wes ignored her, coming towards me. His arms wrapped around me in a hug as he placed a kiss on my cheek.
Grayson growled causing Wes to take a step back. With a chuckle he raised his hands in surrender.
"Not my type remember. No offence Megs."
Grayson's jaw tightened but he nodded, his arms wrapping around me.
He pressed his lips to my ear as he whispered.

"Mine."

My cheeks heated as he let out a throaty chuckle.

"Let's go back to the party, there's cupcakes." Andy said, leading us all towards the packhouse.

I stared out at all my friends, the difference a few months can make. After years of wishing for a mate and a big family and I finally have everything I always wanted.

The perfect mate.

The perfect friends.

I laced my fingers through Grayson's as we followed the others inside.

No more hiding.

This is where I belong.

To be continued...

# *Chapter 1*
## Wes's POV

The ballroom filled with noise as everyone danced with their mates.

Megan laughing as Grayson spun her.

Finally, they had gotten over their problems and accepted each after.

About bloody time if you ask me.

I couldn't help but feel alone as everyone paired up around me.

Sighing, I made my way through the ballroom towards the open bar.

A laugh left my lips as I overheard the conversation of the couple in front of me.

"I told you, I'm Jack Deth, from trancers."

"What are you talking about?"

"It's a movie, before 2000 that's why you haven't watched it."

"Why would I watch some old movie?"

A loud groan is the only reply she got.

My laughing must have pulled their attention because he turned towards me.

As our eyes met the world faded away, leaving only the two of us.

His blonde hair had been slicked back, his bright

green eyes widening as they met mine.

"Mate."

As soon as the word left my lips he froze.

Our gaze disconnected as a tall brunette in a tight black dress with cat ears in her hair wrapped an arm around him.

"Jeremy, what's wrong?"

With a shake of his head, he turned to her, kissing her on the cheek.

"Nothing baby, absolutely nothing."

As he intertwined his hand with hers, he led her away from me, never once looking at me again.

What the hell just happened?

Before I could follow him, Andy grabbed my arm, a smile on her face.

"Hey, there you are. I've been looking everywhere for you."

Forcing a smile on my face I turned my attention on her, trying to avoid looking for my mate.

"You found me what's up?"

Her mouth opened to reply only to close abruptly as her grip tightened painfully on my arm.

The hundreds of candles covering the room suddenly erupted as she let out a thunderous growl.

With wide eyes she looked up at me, her face pale.

"I think my water just broke."

## ABOUT THE AUTHOR

Alexa Phoenix writes sweet, fun, action-packed fantasy. Her characters are clever, fearless, and adventurous but in real life, Alexa spends all her time curled up with a book in her hands, daydreaming. Let's face it. Alexa wouldn't last five minutes in one of her books.

Facebook: AlexaPhoenixFantasyWriter

Tiktok: alexaphoenix23

Instagram: alexaphoenix23

Patreon: Alexaphoenix

# *BOOKS BY THIS AUTHOR*

## Rejecting the Alpha

Amelia

Life has a funny habit of throwing the most peculiar curveballs at you.
Up until now I thought my life was fairly ordinary, but I was so wrong.
After losing my parents two years ago, I found it hard to believe in anything.
Then I met him… Oscar Campbell.
He has changed my entire perspective on life and the world around me. The supernatural world exists and it's closer than any of us realize.
Oscar has awakened something inside of me that I didn't know was there.
I just don't know if I'm ready for this new life.

## Mated

I thought I could hide forever, but fate had other plans.

I can't remember what it feels like to be happy. I'm sure I felt it long ago, back when I thought I was in love. Great husband, great job, great life. Great big lie. At least, that is what my life has turned into now – a series of lies to hide the fact that I am not who I appear to be. The lies keep me hidden and safe… for now.

Surely, my ex-husband would never think to look for me in this sleepy little town. As I settle into my new life, I'm afraid it won't be forever. Could I really give up my job and best friend to go back on the run? Then, I meet Hunter and my world flips upside down.

One night of passion is all I can offer, but he wants more. That's the last thing I need, yet I find myself craving what I can't have. I can't deny this intense attraction that keeps pulling us together like a magnet, and he's not going to take no for an answer.

My heart fills with hope, but it only takes a moment for it to shatter. I'm not the only one keeping secrets, and Hunters are even bigger than my own.

A single mistake is all it takes for me to put his life at risk, and sooner or later my web of lies is going to catch up to me. With everything spiraling out of control, I can only be sure of one thing… my life will never be the same.

Made in United States
North Haven, CT
15 July 2023

39068130R00104